Agai

Translate

an

This edition first publish
lishing, Inc., New York

First published in the U
14 High St, Edinburgh, E

Agamemnon's Daughter
Agamem-nonit by Shtëpi

"The Blinding Order"
Zeri i Rinisë.

"The Great Wall" was f
ume 1 of Vepra (Kadare

1

Agamemnon's Daughter

"The Blinding Order"
Arthème Fayard

English-language tran

The moral rights of th

British Library Catalog
A catalogue record fo
request from the Brit

ISBN 978 1 84767 22

Printed and bound i

www.canongate.net

CONTENTS

TRANSLATOR'S NOTE

This volume contains three stories written at different times, set in different historical periods, but linked to one another and to many other works of Ismail Kadare by recurrent characters, anecdotes, obsessions, and principles.

Agamemnon's Daughter was written in Tirana around the time of the death of Enver Hoxha, who ruled Albania for forty years. The action is placed in the real Tirana of the early 1980s, but its narrative takes us back to the classical roots of Western civilization — and of tyranny. Its sequel, *The Successor*, written many years later, brings the same characters back to life.

"The Blinding Order" was written in 1984 and is set in the Tanzimat, or "reform" period of the Ottoman Empire, in the nineteenth century. It speculates on the uses of terror in a context that is only superficially remote from modern authoritarian regimes.

Mark-Alem, the central character of Kadare's *Palace of Dreams*, makes a fleeting appearance; the main protagonists belong to a branch of the Köprülü clan, whose long history is chronicled throughout Kadare's work.

"The Great Wall" was written in 1993, shortly after Kadare settled in Paris. The bridge built by the Ura family, whose story is told in *The Three-Arched Bridge*, here gives a key to the meaning of the Great Wall of China. We also encounter the horrifying Timur the Lame (Tamerlane), who gives such a stunning conclusion to *The Pyramid*, Kadare's fable of ancient Egypt.

The first of these stories was translated from the French of Tedi Papavrami; the two others, from the French of Jusuf Vrioni. Some amendments have been made to the texts in consultation with the author, particularly with regards to Albanian names and spellings.

D.B.
PRINCETON, N.J., 2006

ABOUT *AGAMEMNON'S DAUGHTER*

Adapted from the publisher's preface to the French edition

In 1986, during one of his infrequent visits to Paris, Ismail Kadare told me that he wanted to leave the manuscripts of two short novels, a story, and some poems in France, as they could not be published in Albania at that time.

He had part of the material with him. "Exfiltration" of literary manuscripts was strictly forbidden under Albanian law, so Kadare camouflaged his text to make it look like an Albanian translation of a work written in the West. He had substituted German and Austrian names and places for Albanian ones, and attributed the works to the West German novelist Siegfried Lenz. Lenz was not unknown in Albania, but not to the extent that people could be sure whether he had written a novel called *The Three Ks*, as Kadare then entitled the novel subsequently known as *L'Ombre* (The Shadow).

Later on, Kadare managed to smuggle more of his manuscripts out of Albania, but because exfiltration remained extremely perilous, he limited his risks by bringing only a few pages on each trip. To get the remainder of the material out of the country, we agreed that the best way was for me to go to Tirana myself. Over two separate trips, I managed to bring all the remaining sheets back to Paris so as to have complete texts of *The Shadow, Agamemnon's Daughter, L'Envol du Migrateur* (A Bird Flying South), and the poems.

The manuscripts were deposited in a safe at the Banque de la Cité in Paris. With the bank's approval, Kadare entrusted me with the key to the safe and gave me authority to open it if and when I thought it necessary.

At that time Ismail Kadare had no greater inkling than anyone else that Albanian Communism would collapse. The deposit of these "dangerous" manuscripts was intended to allow Kadare's publisher, in the event of the writer's natural or "accidental" death, to declare that a previously unknown portion of his work would be published quickly. The revelation of the tone and content of the unpublished works would make it much harder for the Communist propaganda machine to bend Kadare's work and posthumous image to its own ends.

The three prose texts and the poems put into the bank's safe express directly and unambiguously what Kadare thought of the Albanian regime. Previously, he had touched on the matter only indirectly and by allusion, in works like *The Palace of Dreams*, *La Niche de la honte* (The Nook of Shame), and *The Concert*.

The first of these hidden works to appear in France was *The Shadow*, in 1994. It was rewritten to erase its German camouflage, especially noticeable in the earlier part of the novel. Editorial improvements were made to fill gaps that had been left quite intentionally when the work's primary aim had been to get a message across — in the literal sense, across the border separating Albania from the rest of the world.

A Bird Flying South was published later. In Albania, it was published simultaneously in two versions — the original text as smuggled out of Albania and a corrected and edited version, the form in which Kadare wished it to return to Albania.

Agamemnon's Daughter, the third of the manuscripts put into safekeeping, was published in France in 2003 in a translation by Tedi Papavrami from the text written in 1984–1986 without any later changes or revisions. *Agamemnon's Daughter* is the first part of a diptych of which the longer tale, *The Successor*, was written in Paris in 2002. Taken together these two short novels constitute one of the finest and most accomplished of all Ismail Kadare's works to date.

CLAUDE DURAND
PARIS

Agamemnon's Daughter

1

From outside came sounds of holiday music, bustling crowds and shuffling feet — the special medley of a mass of people on their way to the start of a parade.

For perhaps the tenth time in a row, I cautiously pulled the curtain aside. There had been no change in what was to be seen in the street: a slow-moving eddy in the human flood streaming towards the centre of town. Borne on its waves were placards, bouquets of flowers, and portraits of members of the Politburo, just like the ones we saw last year. The politicians' faces looked even more stilted than usual as they jiggled along above the thronging mass of heads and arms. A slip of a placard-bearer's hand sometimes made the painted portraits seem to cast oblique and threatening glances. But even when they came face-to-face, not one of them gave a sign of recognising any other.

I let go of the curtain and realised that I still had the invitation gripped tightly in my hand. It was the first time I had been entitled to sit in the grandstand at the May Day parade, and I still could not quite believe that it really was my own name written on the card. When I first received it, the Party secretary seemed as stunned as I was. It wouldn't be fair to say that the only emotion in his eyes was that of envy: there was also stupefaction. To some extent, that was perfectly justifiable. I wasn't the kind of person who was usually seen at presidium meetings or invited to sit in the stands at public celebrations. Even if (as I later learned) the vice-secretary himself had put my name forward when requested by the local Party committee to suggest people beyond those who came up every year, he was still astonished by the result. Although he had proposed my name, he probably never expected his new list would be approved. "They always ask us for new names," he must have thought, "but it's always the same ones who get invited in the end."

"Congratulations, congratulations," he hissed as he gave me the card, but at the very moment he handed it over, his eyes seemed to me to express something beyond envy and surprise. It hovered within the smile that gave it life, yet it was something separate and different. The right word for it might have been *connivance*. In short, it was an intense, interrogative, and rather sly smile, but sly in that particular well-meaning manner that arises between people who share some secret involvement. His smile seemed to be saying: "This invitation didn't fall off a tree, did it, pal? What job did you do to earn the reward? But who cares anyway! Congratulations, my boy!"

It was so crass I felt myself blush. All the way home, I could not throw off a guilty feeling, as I wondered over and over again: he must be right, but what *did* I do to earn this invitation?

Isolated from the hubbub on the street, the apartment seemed even more silent than usual. Silent and empty. Everyone had left for the starting point of the parade, and my own steps, far from filling the space of the apartment, only emphasised how silent and empty it was. Even the silence and the emptiness had a peculiar quality, as did everything else on a day of that kind.

I was waiting for Suzana. However, the feeling that had burrowed into my chest was not remotely like the anxiety customarily associated with waiting for a woman. It was much more crushing, and no doubt heightened by the music and the unending, exhausting commotion rising from the street. I almost thought that one of the portraits would end up detaching itself from its bearer, then float up to my window, and look inside with its painted frozen stare, and say: "And what are you doing up here? Aha! So that's the reason! You've relinquished your place down there on the reviewing stand to wait for a woman, haven't you?"

"If I'm not there by half past eight, don't wait for me," Suzana had said.

Each time those words came into my mind my eyes glided inexorably towards the couch where our last conversation had taken place. It had been infinitely sad. She'd been half-undressed, and her words had come out the same way — in shreds, with only half their meaning. It was getting harder and harder for her to see me, she said. Papa's career was on the rise . . . Their family was more than ever in the limelight . . . Two weeks before, at the last plenum of the Central Committee, Papa had gone up another rung . . . So it was obvious she would have to make changes to her way of life, to her wardrobe, to the people she saw. Otherwise she might hurt his career.

"Was it he who asked you for that" — I still didn't know what to call *that* — "or did you decide for yourself?"

She looked me in the eyes. "He did," she answered after a pause. "But . . ."

"But what?"

"When he explained it all to me, I saw his point of view."

"Really?"

I thought my eyes must have gone bloodshot, as if someone had thrown sand in my face. Guiltily, she laid her head on my shoulder. She ruffled the hair on the nape of my neck with cold fingers that felt as jagged as broken test tubes.

But why? I wanted to protest. Why just you? The children of the others make the most of it, and lead freer lives, with cars and parties at their villas by the shore . . . I surely would have remonstrated with her along those lines if she hadn't brought up the issue herself. The others usually let their children enjoy more freedom, but her father . . . he really was a different kind of person. Who could tell what was going through his mind? Or was he, on the contrary, completely consistent, and was that not a principle to which he could not allow himself to make an exception? Anyway, if he was standing to the right of the Guide at the First of May parade, it would be all over between us.

I said nothing, and she thought I hadn't quite understood. "Please understand," she sobbed. Given the state of public opinion, her father could not comprehend her having an affair with a young man who was practically engaged to somebody else. Word would leak out, eventually. Especially now, don't you see? It could not fail to.

I didn't know what to reply, but my eyes wandered towards her legs.

"Even for you, it's not wise," she added a minute later.

"*I* don't give a damn."

"Well, you can say that now, but you'll be sorry later on. Especially as you're in the running for the Vienna scholarship."

I carried on staring at the naked parts of her body. To be honest, I wasn't at all sure I was inclined to swap the smooth, white body of this half-girl, half-woman for anything else in the world, including Vienna. The Champs-Elysées of her thighs led all the way to her Arc de Triomphe with its immortal flame . . . I had never before met a woman like Suzana, who kept on smiling with ecstasy during lovemaking, as if she were in the midst of a blissful dream. Her bliss then spread to her cheekbones and spilled onto the white pillow, which even when it was abandoned, after her departure, seemed to keep on glowing faintly in the dark, the way a television screen appears to emit light for a few seconds after you've switched it off. Everything about her betrayed a passionate, serious and fervent attention to the matter of love.

2

I continued to stare at the empty couch while the distant sounds of celebration echoed in my ears. Snatches of our conversations kept coming back to me, but in heightened form, as if intensified by the feeling of loss, like jewels enhanced by a display case. *If on the First of May . . . But you mustn't take it to heart . . . It won't be any easier for me, you know . . . I know what you're going to say . . . But I simply have to make the sacrifice . . . I'll never stop thinking of you . . .*

"The sacrifice," I repeated to myself. "So that's what it's called."

I trusted everything she said, because she always took things seriously and was not in the habit of using words lightly, of dissimulating or putting on airs. If she was convinced that this . . . sacrifice . . . had to be made, there was no point trying to make her change her mind.

In fact, I made no attempt to do so. When she'd

gone, I spent hours pacing the floor and ended up in front of the bookcase. Half dreaming, I took out a book I had just read, and flicked through the pages again. It was *The Greek Myths* by Robert Graves.

I wasn't able then, and have never since been able, to work out by what mysterious path the mechanisms of my mind stripped the word *sacrifice* of its ordinary meaning (*Comrades! The age in which we live demands sacrifices for the sake of oil . . . The sacrifices of our cattle breeders . . .* and so on) and took it far, far back, to its grandiose and blood-soaked beginnings.

This flight into the remotest past was undoubtedly a major turning point for me. From then on, I needed to take only a modest step to see in the sacrifice that Suzana had been talking about something similar to the fate of Iphigenia.

Why had the parallel occurred to me? Because Suzana had used the same word? Because her father, like Iphigenia's, was a high dignitary of the state? Or simply because Graves's book had kept me buried in the world of myth for several days?

As I said, I couldn't fathom the reason why. But I was so feverishly impatient that I didn't even bother to sit down to reread all the pages about the legendary sacrifice of Agamemnon's daughter, from the various more or less plausible hypotheses about what had really prompted the leader of the Greeks to perform that mortal act, down to the speculations about a sham sacrifice, which is to say a show put on for the benefit of the army (with the girl being replaced at the last minute by a fawn), and so on.

What's the point of rereading all that stuff? I wondered. What use can it be? Nonetheless I carried on, avidly ploughing through the heavy tome.

> *To launch the ancient Trojan Wars*
> *They offered up Iphigenia*
> *For the sake of our great cause*
> *I'll carry my darling to the pyre*

Had I invented this verse while wandering like a lost soul around the apartment after I'd put the book back in its place on the shelf, or had I fished it out from a long-sunken memory of something I'd read years before? True sadness often makes me feel sluggish and slow. And that's how I felt then — drowsy, and unable to make things out. For instance, I was quite incapable of putting a name to the author of the poem. Nor was

I up to deciding whether it was I or Suzana's father who was performing the sacrifice. Sometimes it seemed to be me and sometimes him; more likely, it was the two of us in tandem.

The noise from outside had subsided. The street must have emptied. The masses that were going to form the parade had already assembled in the starting area. But this deafening silence was just as hostile and burdensome as the earlier commotion had been. It was a constant reminder that my place was down there amid the festive pandemonium, and not up here all on my own.

Half past eight had come and gone. I could no longer pretend that there was any chance of Suzana turning up. She had always been punctual. I almost regretted her having a quality for which I had so often been thankful, since it now destroyed my last shred of hope. To begin with, I tried to rationalise: being five minutes late is a woman's privilege, even if Suzana had renounced it voluntarily. So I strove to find other reasons for making allowances — traffic jams are so common on celebration days — but instead of mitigating the torture of waiting, the explanations only made it worse. Then came the second set of five minutes, which was even gloomier than the first. Several times I found myself about to go out through the front door.

I decided to wait until a quarter to nine, and then leave for the grandstand, so as not to lose out on both fronts at once. The fear of what might happen if my absence were noticed had up to that point been overshadowed by waiting for her to come, which itself would have given me the strength to wriggle my way out of trouble. (*I lost my way . . . The police closed the road earlier than I expected,* and so on.) If only she had come . . . Whereas now that I had lost her anyway, I had no reason to make things more difficult for myself by not showing up at the parade. Apart from which, I had a good chance of seeing her there, on the grandstand or right next to it, where the offspring of the elite were normally placed.

That last thought finally overcame my hesitation. At five to nine I opened the front door and set off.

3

There was no one on the stairs, and barely any passersby on the street outside. I felt relieved, initially, perhaps because of all the open space. I looked up, as if drawn by the magnetic force of someone else's eyes. Our neighbour was on his balcony, looking as sickly as ever, staring down at the street. I took a step to the side so as to get out of his line of sight. He was reputed to have laughed out loud on the day Stalin died, which brought his career as a brilliant young scientist to a shuddering halt. Many years had passed, of course, but if I remember rightly, a mask of supplication had remained frozen on his face ever since. He couldn't be the only person to have chuckled or laughed among the crowds at the funeral marches that were held that day — for no reason at all, or just for a second, or because their laughter-reflex mechanism had been disturbed, as often happens in such circumstances, but all explanations of such kind were systematically rejected. Every one of them was punished without mercy. Now, many years later, they were still easily identifiable by the wistful appearance they were condemned to wear for the rest of their lives to atone for having once laughed out loud.

You'd better spend your time thinking about the way *you* look! I told myself. My face was probably just as pained as my neighbour's.

As if fearing that my glumness might attract

attention, I took the invitation card out of my pocket and pretended to be studying the verso side, which gave details of how to get into the stands.

Some of the people still in the street must have been in possession of invitations just like mine. You could tell who they were, not only because they were dressed to the nines, but from their attitudes, their postures and their beaming faces. These features distinguished cardholders quite clearly from other pedestrians who had come down into the street in the hope of finding a spot where they could see the parade, or who had got separated from their delegations and were wandering around looking guilty.

Barricade Street, which runs parallel to the Grand Boulevard, was packed with people. A brass band could be heard thumping away in the distance, probably in the square where the stands had been put up. Each time I heard the beat, I walked a little faster, even though it wasn't quite nine o'clock yet and I had no real reason to hurry.

Cardholders were still mixed with other people in the street, but it wasn't long before a filtering device came into view. At the top of Elbasan Road, one of the pavements was open to all, but the other side, the right-hand side, was reserved for invitation-card holders only. The real checkpoint was presumably far-ther down — this was only a preliminary screening. All the same, most of those invited were happy to be separated henceforth from other people, who looked back at them, goggle-eyed.

I continued walking along the left-hand pave-ment, and was just speculating that Suzana would per-haps be in the C-1 stand, where I had my seat, when I bumped into Leka B.

I hadn't seen him for years. Sprightly and beam-ing (though his smile was distinct from the one that seemed to radiate from the little red flags of the day), he gave me a hug and a kiss on each cheek. To be hon-est, I couldn't think why he was so happy to see me again. We'd been pals years before, when I was a law student and he was enrolled at the School of Fine Arts, but not so close that long absence would make either of us miss the other very much.

"How are things?" he asked. "Do you like being a journalist? Lights, cameras, action — the cutting edge, eh?"

"How about you?" I responded. "Still at N?"

"Ah, let's talk about something else!" he said in the same playful tone. "I've not been doing too well. Actually, it wasn't so bad down there, but I did something stupid and got transferred to running amateur theatricals in the sticks."

"Really?"

"Word of honour! I put on a play that turned out to contain no less than thirty-two ideological errors! Can you imagine? Well, that's all ancient history now, and when all's said and done I suppose I got off rather lightly."

My expression must have been hovering between amazement and disbelief, because he added: "You think I'm joking, but I'm telling you the plain truth, honestly."

And he went on in a light-hearted tone entirely devoid of self-pity or spite about his famous thirty-two ideological errors. It was as if he were delighted with the whole business and held it in secret admiration — though you couldn't tell whether what he admired were the people who had had sufficient wisdom and patience to pick out each one of his errors, or himself, as a man who had not committed a trivial blunder or a mere peccadillo, but had engineered a disaster of such magnitude, or else both at the same time.

"So that's how it was," he concluded. "*Twenty-six they were, twenty-six; sand will never cover o'er their graves . . .*"

I've never known what those lines from Esenin were doing there.*

Meanwhile, we had arrived at the crossroads where cardholders were to be finally segregated from commoners. In other circumstances, I would have done anything to avoid flashing my invitation in sight of a comrade still under sentence, but this time I had no option. It had to happen at the precise moment when he asked: "And how are things with you?" As a result, smiling guiltily, and feeling more than a little embarrassed, I took the card from my pocket and blurted out: "As you can see, I've got an invitation to . . . I mean . . ."

I didn't know how to finish my sentence: humorously, or plainly, or by adopting an ironical stance prompted by — well, I don't quite know what. It could have been me, or him, or the whims of fate. But he solved my dilemma by exclaiming brightly: "You've

*The lines are from Sergey Esenin's "Ballad of the Twenty-Six", written in 1924 to commemorate the execution of twenty-six Soviet commissars by a British firing squad in 1918. In Russian:

их было двадцать шесть
двадцать шесть их было
двадцать шесть
их могилы пескам не занесть.

got an invitation! Bravo! Now that's really good news. But shouldn't you hurry up? Aren't you late?"

There wasn't the slightest trace of mockery or repressed envy in his voice or on his face, and I felt sorry for having spent the last twenty-five yards worrying solely about how to get rid of the man.

When I got to the other side of the crossroads, and just before reaching the first line of plainclothes police, I turned around one last time and saw him waving goodbye, still watching me with his sparkling eyes.

I was upset by how nice he had been. However, the suspicion that his behaviour was simply a sign of the implosion of a personality which, for reasons that are hard to explain, takes pleasure in its own downfall (in other circumstances, such a suspicion would have left an unpleasant sensation in the pit of my stomach) was swept away by his good-hearted and happy gesture, which made me all the more relaxed for my encounter with the first line of police.

"ID!"

From the corner of my eye, I watched the inspector's glance going back and forth from my passport photograph to my face, as I tried (for reasons I cannot fathom) to detect in it some sign of disbelief, or ill will, or, on the contrary, respect. A few seconds later, as I left him behind me, I thought I must already be in an advanced state of mental degeneration to worry at all about the impression my face, my name, or my invitation card might make on an insignificant plainclothes policeman I would probably never see again in my life.

Boulevard Marcel Cachin, which connects Elbasan Road to the Grand Boulevard, was packed and at a standstill. The only people who could get through, along the side, were people with invitations, moving individually, as I was, or in small groups. Some of the latter included children carrying toy flags or paper flowers. Others were wearing medals, which cast a yellow gleam on their faces. I was just behind a short, squat man striding boldly forward and holding a little girl by each hand. Both wore ribbons in their hair — one blue, one red — and their charming faces looked as though they had come straight out of a documentary film about official festivities.

The second checkpoint wasn't far from the first. I was expecting it to be stricter, but the procedure was in fact identical, which must have been a disappointment to first-time invitees who were looking forward to a rigorous identity check whose stringency would establish the true value of their invitation. That was completely borne out by the man with the two girls in front of me, who displayed a kind of frustration when, having informed the policemen that the girls were his daughters and that he had their birth certificates with him to prove it, got by way of answer from one of the two cops just a casual "On you go!"

The man was dumbstruck and shook his head as if to say: "You call that a security check?" It was so visible that I almost wanted to get involved and tell him: "Don't worry, there'll be more checks before you get to the grandstand, and they'll be much tighter!"

Boulevard Marcel Cachin is not only particularly wide at this point, it is also curved, so you could look around and get a good view of the various groups of invited guests. They moved forward in line with stilted eagerness, and what with the spring sun above them and the medals and flags they bore, not to mention the nearing sound of the brass band, a warm glow of solidarity arose among people who were otherwise unknown to one another. It wasn't difficult to see why. They had all been singled out by the same hand (the index finger of the state) to participate in the same solemn celebration, and that sealed them in a golden union and made them want to talk to each other, or at least to smirk discreetly. After all, hadn't other people, ordinary people, people not invited, been kept behind the security cordon so as not to bother us any longer with their stunned, over-insistent and interrogative eyes, asking: "So why did they invite you, in particular?"

I felt ashamed to be part of this idyllic and peaceful holiday tableau and was suddenly overcome with a strong desire to see Leka B. again, in whose presence I had at first felt uneasy but who had shown such tact and nobility. Not only had he not allowed the fateful question to emerge, he had demonstrated real warmth, despite having himself been banished for years from all public celebrations.

At the third checkpoint, I came across a Party activist from our own neighbourhood. (Only then did I realise that the plainclothes men were complemented by all sorts of Interior Ministry employees, as well as by volunteers from various neighbourhoods, who were surely also "shadow workers".) In other circumstances, I would have given him a look of scorn, but here, in the radiance of reconciliation emanating from this high mass of togetherness, I was more inclined to favour him with a smile. But he didn't return my greeting; what's more, he pretended not to recognise me. He flicked through my passport looking bored, as if he didn't know me from Adam, although I had bumped into him only the day before at the dairy. Then, without even looking up, he blurted out: "On you go!"

I felt the blood rising in my cheeks from the humiliation, but it did not take long for the man's display of indifference to become the source of an unspecifiable pleasure. The episode proved that even if I was one of the elect on that day, and putting aside the fact that in some insidious and barely perceptible way I was just a little proud of it (despite also feeling a degree of shame for the same reason), I had not become an indistinguishable part of the elite or, to be more precise, of the upper circle's dark side. That's why our neighbourhood activist had looked me over with his evil eye and had probably muttered under his breath: "What's this guy doing here? Who the hell selected such a nonentity to sit in the grandstand?"

That's all it took to make me begin to watch out for signs of hostility. And the nearer I got to the Grand Boulevard, the more I noticed them. But I hadn't seen anything yet. Just when I was least expecting it, when I had come to believe that I could now be pricked only by hauteur (people who were accustomed to getting invited every year would naturally take exception to newcomers), and that I had nothing to fear apart from a single enemy called jealousy, since the other, nagging, questioning foe ("So what did you do to earn the invitation, eh?") had been cordoned off by our common condition on that score, since we were all more or less in the same boat, it was precisely at that point that the snake reared its ugly head higher than ever. Two youngish men in raincoats, with the kind of faces that made you think you'd seen them before somewhere, but who knows where, looked me up and down from the side as they crossed my path. I got the impression that their glances had a touch of sarcasm about them. I turned around to make sure they weren't focusing on me, that I was simply a trifle paranoid, but I saw to my alarm that it really was me they were glaring at. Not only did they carry on ogling me, they were also whispering in each other's ears while the smiles on their lips twisted into something close to a sneer.

I went red in the face. The automatic reflex of hurrying on past suddenly went into reverse, and I almost stopped to shout at them: "What's making you cluck like a pair of hens? What makes you think I don't have my own suspicions about you two as well!"

I didn't do anything of the sort, of course, but kept on going and tried to forget about them, to no avail. I calmed down slightly when we got separated by a good-humoured group, in the middle of which I could make out the squat father with his red- and blue-beribboned girls.

I was still carrying on under my breath my argument with the two young men. What gives you a monopoly on the right to suspect people? When all is said and done, what makes you any more qualified than I am in that domain?

That's what I muttered to myself, but, who knows why, I felt that nothing would ever wipe the snigger off their faces. However, I suddenly thought I had found the key to the mystery: the first person to entertain suspicion wins the match. The suspected person, despite probably being innocent, is always on the defensive simply from having been slow off the mark.

What a crazy idea! I protested inwardly. As a last resort, I tried to recall what I had read about collective guilt and so on. But nothing came back to me.

The beribboned girls ahead of me had started demanding something in twittering voices. The father dealt with them patiently, sugaring his answer with affectionate nicknames for each of his daughters.

An ideal paterfamilias, holding his daughters by the hand, on a sunny socialist First of May. A pretty picture, I said to myself. But tell me — who's paying for this idyllic scene? Who did *you* put away to get your place in the sun?

I was the first person to be surprised by my own outburst of anger. But surprise didn't stop me from looking around with hatred streaming from my eyes. I'd turned into a terrorist, driven to ecstasy by the sight of blood, who starts to fire indiscriminately into the crowd. Since that was the way things were, I preferred to shoot first, and take my punishment later.

He who lingers is lost.

4

Soon thereafter, I felt my forehead glazing over with cold sweat. I'd lost sight of the two guys in raincoats and of the model family in blue and red ribbons. I was moving forward among strangers whom I had shamelessly attacked, at whom I had flung whole handfuls of mud without thinking for a moment that nothing stopped them from doing the same to me.

The Grand Boulevard was not far off now. Haven't you got anything on your own conscience? I asked myself. Six months previously, as I came out of a local Party inquiry where we'd heard the charges against us,

I'd asked myself that question for the first time. Now I shook my head again, as I had then. No, there was no stain of that kind on my conscience! Although I had been the unwitting cause of two colleagues in a neighbouring office being sentenced to relegation to some godforsaken hole, I was not guilty. Quite the opposite: you could say that their stupidity had very nearly caused my own ruination. "You are at a meeting of a committee of the Party, and you should know that at meetings of Party committees, lying is forbidden!" the secretary shouted as he looked straight into our eyes. "You there!" he said, pointing at me. "Where was it that you heard the perfidious insinuation that gossip and tittle-tattle about the fall of such and such a leader, far from emanating from the petit-bourgeois element in our society and from there seeping into the minds of the people, had been manufactured by the state itself — that is to say, according to your story, by a secret bureau set up for the specific purpose of paving the way for the actual fall of said leader?"

I had never in all my life felt so uncomfortable. My office partner, who was gaping open-mouthed on the other side of the room, had indeed told me the story, but what I did not know then was that he had already confessed everything. I replied point-blank, with a strange confidence, which I allowed to take over for the seconds and minutes it lasted, that I had indeed read such a theory in a book about Czechoslovakia after the Soviet invasion. The secretary's eyes looked right through me, but as I spoke I managed to convince myself that I really had read something like that in a book. What helped me make such a show of sincerity was that I genuinely had just finished skimming through a book about Czechoslovakia.

I don't know what it was that the secretary liked about my answer. It would have been only fair of him to lean toward my partner's version, since he'd taken the risk of baring himself, and thus to treat my story with scepticism. But the opposite happened. Without giving them time to justify themselves ("Thank goodness," they told me later on, "that's exactly what we wanted to avoid having to do!"), he accused my office colleagues of being dangerous chatterboxes, sinister idiots, liars and megalomaniacs who thought they understood politics when in fact they didn't have a clue. Incurable gossips who lacked all sense of responsibility, who transposed anything they heard about the horrible truths of bourgeois countries onto our own fine socialist way of life, and so on. Whereas I got off with one of those criticisms that sounded more like praise. In other words, I should have taken greater care to separate subjects such as those involved in the present erroneous comparison, to ward off any confusions that could give rise to conversations such as those under consideration, especially if I ever talked of such things in the hearing of brainless twits who were as politically naïve as my two colleagues.

"Make yourself scarce now! Get out, and remember, not a word of this to a living soul, you understand?" Those were the secretary's last words to me. For a long time I found his behaviour and the sudden conclusion of the case rather puzzling. Did it come from some cog in the machine suddenly changing direction and causing a whole string of illogicalities to ensue? Or was it that the secretary simply seized upon the introduction of an alien element like Czechoslovakia to bring the whole thing to a rapid end? Maybe it was even simpler than that. He'd had a lot of problems to deal with at the time, what with criticisms from above about the shortfall in the Economic Plan, and so on, and maybe he'd just wanted to get an awkward piece of business over and done with as quickly as possible.

He looked on me almost with kindness, simply because I had taken this burden off his shoulders. As I left the room, I thought he was about to put his avuncular hand on my shoulder, just as I'd seen done so many times in films made in the "New Albania" studios. And although his hand did not actually materialise, I spent many days wondering what people would now say about me. That was inevitable, as I was the only one of the three people caught up in this business to get off without a scratch. It was a stroke of pure luck that, before they left for the back of beyond, the other two kept on saying to all and sundry that I had nothing to do with it, that they had only themselves to blame, and that they were very glad the story stopped there, because it could have turned out much worse.

Later on, whenever my mind wandered back to this episode, I was more and more struck by the words: "Make yourself scarce now! Get out, and remember, not a word of this to a living soul!" The secretary's hurry to close the case, his gratitude towards me, and especially his inclination to treat it as mainly a matter of harebrained idiots and boastful liars, gradually clarified what had at first seemed a real puzzle. There really wasn't any mystery, even less an illogical chain of events caused by a loose cog in the machine. And it had nothing to do with the secretary being exhausted by an overheavy workload. It was a device intended to nip the rumour in the bud. The rumour was of an

especially dangerous sort that the state had every reason to stop before it started. That was why, when the
sentence was made public, the real charge was not
mentioned at all, and the two men were sent down
officially for professional lapses of the kind anyone
could be accused of at any time.

It would have been more logical for the state to
turn a blind eye and let the two men go scot-free. But
who knows which cog was whizzing away on its own
and still demanding a punishment at any cost . . . Unless something else was going on that I could not figure out.

That was what was chaotically floating around in
my mind as I came up to the Grand Boulevard. After
a lapse of several months, I was once again worried
that what had really happened would look suspicious
to some people. After all, anyone who knew me would
be quite right in finding my presence in the grandstand suspicious. I myself had wondered two or three
times whether or not I had served as an unwitting tool
to dig my colleagues' graves a little deeper. After all, I
was the person responsible for their having been accused of mistakenly confusing revisionist waywardness
with the realities of socialism . . . Not to mention what
they might think if they both saw me today on their

television screens! They would probably think: "We believed he was getting us off the hook, but apparently he must have been digging our grave even deeper to wind up with such a lavish reward!"

They would have done better not to give me this invitation, I reflected. Or I would have been better off not coming, as Suzana and I had agreed . . . Suddenly all the pain of her absence hit me as heavily as the lid of a tomb. Oh Lord! I sighed bitterly. Too many burdens to bear all at once!

Where the two boulevards intersected there was another checkpoint, which was stricter than the others. But I had now stopped worrying about them. A secret hope that the cops would find something out of order on my invitation and make me turn back made my heart beat faster as I waited at each security check.

No such luck! In some areas of life, delays, oversights and sloppiness just don't arise. Issuing official invitations was one of them.

Both sides of the Grand Boulevard were packed with people. That was where most of the invited guests were placed. That's exactly how it was written on their cards: "Left or right side of grandstand". Whereas we who had seats still had to plough our way through this seething ocean. I'd already aroused suspicion and jealous pangs by getting this far, but when people understood I was supposed to go even higher, how much more animosity would be coming my way! Anyway, the real nightmare would presumably begin only at that point. I imagined that when people realised what I was set for, they would grab my coat tails, haul me back down, and raise the alarm.

Instinctively, I slowed my pace to deflect any suspicion I might have aroused by marching forward too eagerly. I wanted to look like someone who, in common with all the other recent arrivals, was simply bent on finding the best spot.

Shortly after, I realised that the pavement had been transformed into a promenade. Since the best seats for watching the parade had long been staked out, everyone not yet ensconced was sauntering up and down, running into old acquaintances, greeting them with guffaws, and so on. Here and there you could make out a glinting medal. On rare occasions it was a star of the Order of Heroes of Socialist Labour. Seen from outside or by the goggle-eyed people who'd just been watching us make our way to the platform, the place must have looked like a corner of paradise. A contingent of the Socialist elite in glorious May Day sunshine, right next to the heavenly choir . . .

Well, I thought to myself, even if none of that is true, even if there's not a sliver of paradise here, maybe it's not exactly the total opposite either, not the hell on earth I had imagined it would be . . . Things were probably much simpler, and my fevered mind was making everything seem blacker than it was.

Slightly reassured, I looked at my watch. It was almost half past nine. Maybe it was time to go up into the grandstand. Out of the human mass on the street, a line had formed and was making its way in orderly fashion in that direction, and to my great surprise no one betrayed any sign of guilt, shame or hesitation. On the contrary, most people were holding their invitation cards in plain sight, with a touch of pride, and stopped to look at them close up or at arm's length as they pretended to be checking where their seats were (as if they hadn't already done that at home a dozen times over!) and then, with serious faces, moved straight ahead.

I was about to join the line without any further self-doubts. After all, they had been coming here for years, and I was discovering it all for the first time. For the last time too, in all probability . . .

"Keep moving! Keep moving!" a voice bawled from the nearby loudspeaker, as if to bolster my resolve. I thought that a smile was about to break out on my face, but it never got that far. For on my right, in a group of quite young fellows, most of whom I knew (some were employees of *Zeri i popullit*, the daily newspaper, and others worked at the Central Committee), I saw G. Z.

I can't imagine what else in that crowd could have brought me back so sharply to the very worst that the world has to offer, to its most deathly and abominable manifestation. A sombre chasm, then a great fall, then a desperate jerk to try to escape at any cost from the chaos . . . But wasn't that the ancient tale of Bald Man Falling?

One night as he was walking in the dark, Bald Man fell into a hole and kept on falling and falling right down to the netherworld . . .

5

I had known G. Z. since the time he was employed at our TV station, and I'd never thought very much of him. His complexion was grey, but more sickly than pale, probably a symptom of his lack of personal hygiene which, combined with his unwashed shirts and self-proclaimed taste for plain dressing (which was more likely just miserliness) and with his constant harping on his orphan status at meetings (*Comrades, I never had a father or a mother. No! The Party is my only family*), which itself provided an inexhaustible supply of emotion for delegates but never failed to exasperate one of our colleagues no end (*What unadulterated bullshit!* he would grumble. *It's only his mother who's dead, his father's alive and as fit as a fiddle. Given the circumstances, why doesn't he say the Party is his substitute mummy?*), his whole personality and history corresponded in sum to what in relatively polite language is called a pile of shit.

But that was presumably where the roots of his career were planted. Because a career, as one of my friends often liked to say, is built not just on enthusiasm and energy, but on some special gift that has to be such an integral part of the individual in question as to be barely distinguishable from his genes. That gift, which in others may take the outward appearance of a heart of stone, natural perversity, infinite servility, or God knows what else, manifested itself in dull-witted G. Z. in his ostensible orphan identity, which for reasons unknown persuaded our leaders that there was nothing he was not prepared to trample in the mud if he one day should be asked to do so.

Indeed he had already covered quite a lot of ground. At the Broadcasting Service to begin with, then at the National Theatre, where, people said, he was highly valued. You could see right away that he had an inextinguishable hankering for the higher slopes . . . But one night, one of his relatives was arrested.

One night, Bald Man fell all the way down to the netherworld . . .

It had never occurred to me that a nonentity like G. Z. could be the pretext for likening an old folktale to what was, ultimately, an ordinary event in the lives we led. But as our office boss was wont to ask, isn't it true that repulsive insects bring to mind, more often than you might expect, fine and lofty thoughts?

After his fall, Bald Man strove with all his might to find the way and the means to clamber back to the upper world. He wore himself out searching every corner, until an old man whispered the solution in his ear. There was an eagle that could fly all the way up by the sheer strength of his wings — but on one condition. Throughout the flight, the raptor would need to consume raw meat. Bald Man didn't think that would be a problem.

(What had they asked G. Z. to supply in return

for his place in the upper world? Whose flesh had he given?)

G. Z. was in a state of utter turmoil for days and nights on end. He spent his time going from one office to another bad-mouthing his cousin, repudiating him, swearing he would wring his neck with his own two hands, if only the Party would put him to the test! People who knew him better than I said that the man's agitation was not just for show. By their account, it sounded more like proof of integrity, which to some extent justified his attitude. But when I heard about it, I thought it a perfect example of the baseness of human nature.

He traipsed all over the place and wore himself out hunting for a solution: his servility and eagerness to crawl were like a drug. The inexhaustible supply of devotion to the Party that such a person found himself able to summon up may have come as more of a surprise to himself than to anyone else. He raced from corridor to corridor, from office to office, until someone finally showed him how to climb out of the hole he was in. That someone knew someone who . . . on one condition . . . G. Z. didn't think that would be a problem.

The precise nature of what base act G. Z. had committed was never disclosed.

In the netherworld, Bald Man obtained a supply of meat before climbing on the eagle's back, and so the flight back to the upper world began. Now and again in the course of flight the eagle asked to be fed, and so Bald Man cut him a piece of the meat he had brought.

G. Z. had been banned from publishing his own work, but he was still a member of the National Theatre. He'd already told people close to him that his case would soon be resolved. In two or three weeks, at the outside four or five, his own prospects would be irrevocably disconnected from his cousin's plight. Especially as he wasn't a first cousin anyway . . . But the matter was not resolved within two to three weeks, or in four or five.

The eagle's flight to the upper world was taking much longer than Bald Man had expected. All the meat had disappeared down the bird's gullet. Bald Man looked on the sinister abyss with fear in his soul as the eagle kept flying around and around. The pit beneath seemed bottomless.

"Kroa, kroa!" croaked the eagle, for it was his way of asking for food. Bald Man shivered with horror.

What could he give him now? For the old man had warned him: if the beast doesn't get his ration of meat when he asks for it, then you're in for a very great fall.

"Kroa!" the eagle croaked once more. On the spur of the moment, Bald Man dug the knife into his forearm and cut out a piece of his own flesh.

We never learned exactly what G. Z. did in the week when they finally put him to the test. All we heard about, to begin with, was that he'd set a trap at a Party meeting for a fashionable young playwright: he'd sent some of the latter's poems about the Guide (obtained with the help of a bodyguard who was a friend of his) to the Guide's own children, with a letter complaining that for well-known reasons publication of the poems had been forbidden. And then came the main thing: the arrest of a young scriptwriter on the basis of an analysis (more surely, of the denunciation) that G. Z. had made of the man's script.

I rubbed my forehead to ease my migraine. No, the story of Bald Man feeding the infernal eagle with his own flesh could no longer be made to fit the story of G. Z. at this point. That man would have been quite incapable of feeding an eagle with flesh he'd not cut from someone else. Bald Man's self-mutilation gave the folktale a tragic turn and a funereal grandeur that were completely inapplicable to G. Z. and his ilk. Not one of them would give up a single hair on his head to save anyone else. Whereas Bald Man . . .

"Kroa, kroa!" the eagle croaked again after a while, and his passenger had to stick the blade into his thigh to cut out another piece of flesh. He carried on, looking glumly down into the inky blackness of the pit. Then he gazed in turn at all the different parts of his body that he would have to part with when the eagle asked for more. Lord, every morsel would be just as painful as any other!

The eagle flew on endlessly through the ice-cold dark. Now and again he croaked, and Bald Man took a slice out of this or that part or place in his body. It seemed the journey would never end. Sometimes he thought he could see a faint glimmer of light in the distance, but it was only a hallucination invented by his weary eyes.

"Kroa, kroa . . ." He had to start cutting pieces off his chest as the rest of his body was now almost down to the bone. Once again he thought he saw daylight in the far distance . . .

It's not known if Bald Man was still alive when the eagle came out into the upper world. People say that locals who happened to be around at the time couldn't believe their eyes when they saw a huge black bird carrying a human skeleton on its back. "Hey! Come quick, there's something incredible to see!" they called out to each other. "An eagle has brought up a dead man's bones . . ."

6

I had lost sight of G. Z. and didn't want to think about him anymore. He wasn't the only one who had torn out living flesh so as not to fall to the bottom of a pit, with no means of climbing back up. There were others . . . Maybe I was one of them. We'd taken a path not really knowing where it would lead, not knowing how long it was, and while still on our way, realising we had taken the wrong road but that it was too late to turn back, every one of us, so as not to be swallowed up by the dark, had started slicing off pieces of our own flesh.

I continued to massage my forehead. The noise of the crowd all around me had merged entirely with the sound of the band. Meanwhile I was far, far away, in a dark and bottomless shaft, where we all sat astride our eagles, circling whichever way the wind cared to push us . . .

"Well, well! Fancy seeing you here! But you look as though you have your head in the clouds . . . Anyway, Happy First of May, all the same!"

It was my uncle. Though delighted to see me, he couldn't mask his surprise. His eyebrows stayed raised and his eyes expressed unabated astonishment all the time he was speaking to me, as if he could not come to terms with the fact that I really was there.

"He's a nephew of mine, he works in the broadcasting service," he said, with no small pride, to a knot of acquaintances.

I did not like my uncle. Each time we had met these past years, we got into an argument, since we held opposing views on every subject: on the incompetence of managers, on shortages, on Stalin, television programming, the Kosovo question, and so on. I don't recall our ever having agreed about anything. Even the weather, which usually helps bring the most unwilling opponents onto common ground, gave rise to clashes between us. He liked hot climates and I preferred cool ones. He never failed to draw ideological conclusions from this difference of taste:

"It's obvious that you prefer the climate of Europe, since it's your model in every respect!"

"So what model should I have?" I used to retort.

"Bangladesh? The Far East? Skanderbeg fought for a quarter of a century to snatch Albania out of Asia and to bring it into the European fold. What have you and your friends been doing? You've never stopped trying to push Albania back again!"

That's when we usually got into another spat about the Chinese, and then things would really heat up. He would call me a liberal and a revisionist, and would foam at the mouth when he saw these epithets no longer awed me. He would try to come up with other, nastier epithets, but as he couldn't find any (in his eyes, those were already the worst he could think of), he just kept repeating them.

"Unreconstructible revisionist! Hopeless liberal! . . ."

For my part, I just called him a China-lover and observed how lucky we were that countries could not be mounted on wheels, otherwise we would already have moved to somewhere near the Gobi Desert or Tibet. "Down there you'd feel safe, I'm sure!" I added. "Or wouldn't that be far enough from accursed Europe for you?"

We'd fought about the Chinese when our country's diplomatic love affair with Beijing was at its peak, but we argued even more when the affair was broken off. When news first went around that trouble was brewing, he dropped in at our place, looking fraught, with furrowed brow. "On a number of points, my boy, I think you were not entirely wrong; those Chinese weren't all they claimed to be . . ." However, on the day that obviously should have been the occasion of our reconciliation, our most violent dispute arose. That was when I first called him brain-dead, and he threatened to denounce me.

To be honest, I had jumped at the opportunity of renewing hostilities as soon as he said he was surprised that I — champion Sinophobe that I was — hadn't seemed happier on hearing the announcement that relations with Beijing were being broken off.

"Good Lord!" he said. "You really are a strange one, my boy, you're a real killjoy. You've been griping about the Chinese for years, but now that things are turning your way, you're not jumping for joy but sulking."

That's when I lost my temper. "So why should I be jumping for joy?" I screamed at him. "We should be weeping instead. But you won't understand that, seeing that you're already brain-dead!" I was really on the rampage. We were breaking off relations with the Chinese not because of their atrocities, but for the opposite reason — because they were on the point of giving them up. Whereas Albania would curl up and die if it had to give up being cruel! We'd connived with the Chinese for the sole purpose of inventing new horrors. Now they were moving in another direction, we couldn't think of anything better to do than leave them behind! It was enough to make you tear your hair out! But then, we'd always behaved that way. We'd been friends with the Yugoslavs when they were ultra-orthodox, but we'd turned on them as soon as signs of a thaw came from Belgrade. We'd been allies of the Soviets during the worst period of Stalinist terror, but had turned our backs on them the moment they began to show a modicum of civilisation. And it was the same old story with the Chinese. All other countries had ended up turning away from evil and obscurantism. But Albania remained their last bastion! We'd become the high priests of calamity and the shame of the universe. Was there any other country like ours? Accursed, O thrice-accursed land!

He was flabbergasted by what he heard, and he stared at me with wide eyes filled with hatred and horror. He tried to butt in two or three times, but his mouth had probably gone dry. Only when I got to declaim "accursed land" did he manage to articulate: "I am going to report you!"

"Go ahead!" I responded. "But don't forget that the shadow of my fall will affect you, too . . ."

At that point, as he usually did in such circumstances, he took out a box of pills and swallowed a dose of nitroglycerin.

That was our next-to-last quarrel. The last one arose over a slogan in one of the Guide's speeches: *We shall eat grass if we have to but we will never renounce the principles of Marxism-Leninism!* I told my uncle I thought the statement was the height of absurdity and deeply offensive to the nation's dignity.

"What are the principles for whose sake we are supposed to turn into cows? What use could they possibly be to us then? To glorify our shepherd?"

He went pale, and his jaw began to quiver. He didn't know what to say.

"Well, go on, then! Give us an answer!" I pursued. "What use could we make of principles whose purpose is to turn us into cattle, like a flock of Circes?"

As I was speaking, my mind was wondering whether that was not in fact the secret wish entertained by the Guide — to bring humanity down to the

level of a herd of herbivores . . . meek and dumb . . .
all in the name of the principles of Marxism-
Leninism . . . Lord, what a pantomime!

"Do you have any idea of the terrible joke that's
being played on us?" I went on at the top of my lungs.
"The rest of the world is moving on and making the
most of life, whereas we are supposed to sacrifice ourselves for the sake of some so-called principles? What
have the principles of Marxism-Leninism got to do
with Albania, since, as you yourself agree, the rest of
the world has given them up for good? By what right
must our martyred, pauperised countrymen remain
the last defenders of principles they didn't even in-
vent? In the name of the future of humanity? Do you
mean to say that because in London and Paris and Vienna and so on people have followed the primrose
path and ended up wallowing in luxury, music and
self-indulgence, we Albanians have to sacrifice ourselves and eat grass for the salvation of their souls?
Really! What a farce!"

"Stop!" he finally managed to blurt out. "You are
rotten to the core, and totally incapable of understanding these things! You can't understand that it
would not matter one iota if Albania were wiped off

the face of the earth so long as the ideas of the Guide
were assured of an eternal future!"

I was struck dumb by this argument, which I
hadn't heard before. (I later learned that it had been
issued by the minister of the interior during a secret
meeting of Party cadres.)

He took my silence for defeat, and interpreted it
as a surrender. He looked me up and down for a moment with a triumphant glance, until I returned to the
attack, from an angle that took him completely by
surprise.

"What you've just come out with is the most
heinous accusation ever made against the Guide,"
I said.

"Accuse the Guide? Me?" He grinned. "Anyway,
who's talking about the Guide?"

"You are!" I replied. "The mere fact of positing an
alternative between 'Albania' and the 'Guide' is the
same as making a grave accusation against the latter.
It comes down to saying that it has to be one or the
other, that there's no room for both in this world. In
other words, *mors tua vita mea.*"

"I didn't say that. Don't twist my words!" he
shouted.

"But that *is* what you said!" I answered. "You said it explicitly: may Albania be wiped off the face of the earth so that the ideas of the Guide may go marching ever on!"

All of a sudden, my head was a mass of confusion. Maybe that was the Guide's true secret: to wipe this infuriating country called Albania off the face of the earth, this nation of paupers forever getting under his feet, whom he had to feed and rule over all these years! Once they'd been got rid of, turned into thin air, how clean it would be, how spotless! A country that had died, but was kept alive in the ideas and books of its Leader. How convenient, too! No awkward reality to contradict you, not a trace of evidence of the crimes that had been committed. Nothing but his books, his ideas, his *lumières* . . .

"I never said that!" my uncle kept on screaming. "You've twisted my words, you're the devil incarnate!"

Our argument was winding down and about to end with its invariable routine exchange: I'll report you . . . Go on, and the shadow will fall on you . . . Then the dose of heart medicine, and so on. Except that this time, it was I who said: "I'm going to report you." I went further. Egged on by my own excess of sarcasm (I'd noticed that sarcasm calmed me down, especially when it hit my uncle right in the eye), I added: "I'm going to report you, but it's a damn nuisance, as the shadow will fall on me, too."

At this point he completely lost his temper, and our fight ended in a particularly grotesque scene. Each screamed he would denounce the other, that the shadow of the other's fall would fall on him too, then we went through the ritual of the pills — but to his surprise and to mine, I snatched the box and downed a pill myself, then ran off like a scalded cat.

Memories of these episodes must have also come into my uncle's mind in some form or another because the amazement you could read in his eyes just kept on growing. But there was also a note of triumph in his expression: *At last! Now you're on the right road, my boy! You snorted and snarled to your heart's content, but now you've come back into the fold!*

"So they issued you an invitation?" he queried, patting me on my shoulder. "Congratulations! Congratulations! I'm delighted for you."

If we'd been alone he would probably have said: "Cut the niceties. Now tell me just how . . . ?" But though he said nothing, his whole attitude — the way he looked at me, the pat on the shoulder copied from "New Albania" movies — got the message across maybe even more effectively.

I started to shake his hand in farewell, but he went on cheerfully: "What, are you leaving? Stay here, my dear boy. It's a good spot, you can see everything."

"Well, it's just that . . ."

The instinct for self-preservation would have held me back from telling him that I had a seat in the grandstand, but as I couldn't think what else to say, I had to let him know.

His attitude switched entirely. As if what he'd seen in my hand was not an official invitation card but a death announcement.

He took it from me, or rather, snatched it out of my fingers with the angry swoop of a bird of prey. Greedily, sceptically, his fierce eyes pecked every word on the card looking for some unforgivable error. He hung on to it for a while (I thought I could see his hands shaking) and drips of perspiration glazed his forehead. His face, his whole being, even the medals that I thought I heard making an ominous clinking sound, seemed to be saying: There's been a misunderstanding! A misunderstanding! You! Admitted to the grandstand! You with your sick ideas about management, about Stalin, about free trade . . . The look in his eyes was a mixture of suspicion and spite. I would have sworn that if he could have, he would have called the appropriate authorities on the spot to report the event, or rather to stab me in the back, as was only right and proper. *It's true he's my brother's son, but the Party has to come first, yes?*

"Are you two having an argument?" one of his friends asked jovially.

"Er . . . no, not at all . . ."

At last my uncle gave the card back to me. His face looked utterly flabby and worn. Then, in spite of his lingering bewilderment, a devilish gleam came into his eyes. They narrowed and narrowed until his glance was as sharp as a knife. He flashed it at me with an intensity that seemed unbearable. Awareness of his own superiority unconsciously reshaped his face, which a few seconds before had looked so defeated. The question I feared the most was plain to see in all its cruelty: What did you do to earn this invitation? And on its tail the sarcastic implication: You played at being a little hero as long as you could, didn't you, but in the end you realised that there is no other way.

It was my turn to have sweat on my brow.

You may enjoy denigrating us day and night, but we

did at least earn these invitations honestly, like we earned everything else. We mean what we say, and this is our celebration. But you don't think that way. So what are you doing here?

Unless what made you so bitter was not being able to rise to the very top? Then at the first opportunity you denied what you are, and sold yourself body and soul in order to clamber up the greasy pole. You must have been really good at it, my boy, because you've not only caught up, but overtaken the lot of us! Yes, you must have done something really special! Well, I guess that's how these kinds of things happen. Now it's our turn to give you a wide berth, my boy!

I was pretty sure that that was what was swirling around in his head, whereas I was overcome with an irresistible desire to shout out loud: No! I've done nothing of the sort you're mulling over in your squalid little pigeon-brain, you stupid old fogey! On the contrary! An hour ago I was fully prepared to swap this invitation for an assignation. If only you knew who she was . . . But what could a retarded oaf like you understand about that?

I was still gripping the invitation card in my hand when he came out with: "Go on up, you're going to be late . . ."

His eyes, like his words, were as cold as ice. Alternative expressions such as "Be gone, evil scourge!" would have been no harsher.

"Shove off yourself, you old nitwit, and take your rusty old medals with you!" I muttered to myself as I moved off without even shaking his hand.

Shortly thereafter, I found myself among the small trickle of people wending their way up to the stands. We were assailed from all sides by furtive, sideways glances charged with such a particular blend of envy, admiration and bitterness that it twisted mouths into smiles that could just as well be called anti-smiles.

I would have done better to tear up the invitation and never shown my face here. Ah, Suzy, what have you brought me to?

7

My sorrow at losing her pained me cruelly. Suzy . . . That's how I'd said her name in my head every time I'd feared she would drop me. It was more apt to sear you, just as it seemed a better reflection of the pride of a daughter of the elite. Ah, Suzy, what have you brought me to, I repeated. You really picked the right day for breaking up!

I knew that the pain of losing her would be long-lived, but on that day it was almost unbearable.

As I moved forward, with my presumably glum face contrasting with the festive mood all around me, I saw a silhouette I recognised, barely a few yards ahead of me. It was Th. D., the painter, apparently on his way, like me, to a seat in the grandstand. He was holding his younger daughter by the hand. (Well, well: where had the blue and red ribbons gone?)

Probably in thrall to the notion that I would be less noticeable in his shadow, I elbowed through the crowd to get as close as possible to him. Perhaps I might also take advantage of the legitimacy of his presence here. In his case, at least, the reasons why he had a place in the grandstand were known to all.

As I proceeded, I studied the expression on his face. Apart from my own, his was the only blank face in the whole junketing crowd. That's the way he always looked on television broadcasts of the various public ceremonies where I'd seen him appear. It was likely he'd earned the right to scowl in public long ago. Indisputably a far more precious asset than all the fees he must earn.

I knew of no one else in the whole country who was simultaneously considered privileged and persecuted. It sometimes happened that these two adjectives were both applied to him in the same after-dinner conversation, and even by the same speaker. Everyone agreed nonetheless that the nature of his relations with the state were shrouded in mystery. There was talk of him being criticised, even of his being accused of the kind of grievous error that can break a man for good, but, except on one occasion at a Party Plenum, it had all taken place behind closed doors. Then, when his fall was fully expected — *He's going to get it in the neck* and *He's untouchable* were equally popular topics for after-hours gossip — his face suddenly reappeared on some platform or other, looking as morose as ever.

What had he paid for such immunity? For, like all of us, he too must have had his eagle, probably a more terrifying one than any other, to keep him going through the night.

People said lots of other things about him in café conversations and after-dinner talk. He was rumoured to arouse a great deal of jealousy in the upper echelons, not to say at the topmost rung of the ladder, especially because he exhibited abroad. Among the other observations that he provoked, what people disagreed about most was the role he might or might not play in the life of the nation. Some asserted that he already did play a role by means of his work; others said not. We should expect more, much more of him, they insisted, all the more so because he could rest assured that nobody would dare try to bring him down. He was well aware he was untouchable. So why didn't he take advantage of it?

"You're the one who says they can't get at him," another would reply. "In the light of day, they're powerless, I grant you that. But who can be sure that nothing could happen to him under cover or behind the scenes? An automobile accident, for instance, or a dinner that just happened to be off, and then, next morning, a splendid funeral, and *finita la commedia!* I'd go so far as to say that the irritation you can feel now and then on his account is there for him to hear the message: *Aren't you grateful to be still alive? What more do you want?*"

"Ah, yes, I hadn't thought of that," the first speaker replied, aghast.

That's what was said about the man, but as I walked just behind him, what was especially on my mind was that no one could have said that he'd earned the right to be seated in the stands by performing some ordinarily sordid act. So I kept on convincing myself blindly that I was taking advantage of some sliver of his immunity on the way to my seat, which was turning into something more like a way of the cross.

He passed a number of senior figures in the government (well, that's what they looked like, to judge by their suits) and each in turn chucked his daughter's cheek.

"That one looks after our newspapers," he told his daughter with a smile, "and he's our foreign minister." He could have been showing her new toys.

At any rate, that's the impression it made on me. Everything he said was imbued with the kind of ease that comes only from elevation — from the great height whence a man who already knows he is immortal can look down and comment upon the temporal affairs of this world.

"Who's higher up, the foreign minister or the minister of the interior?" the little girl asked as the pair of them moved farther away from me.

I tried to catch up, to hear the answer.

"Well, now . . . how can I put it? Interior affairs are unmistakably the most important."

"But foreign ones are much more attractive!" the little girl protested.

He laughed.

"Do you mean dresses?" he asked. "You're right!"

We were now almost underneath the grandstand. A security check far more stringent than the last awaited us.

I took my invitation card out of my pocket again and went up to the barrier. I don't know why, but I thought I could hear a buzzing in my inner ear.

"ID!"

"Oh, of course. Sorry."

A few yards farther on came the start of another zone, with an entirely different atmosphere. It was full of diplomats looking for their seats, delegations from abroad and TV camera crews.

I strode easily across the few yards that separated me from it. I felt as if my whole appearance betrayed distraction, particularly the expression on my face, or, to be more precise, the smile that must have been on it. I was shown the access route to the C-1 stand, which I instantly forgot, until someone else showed it to me again. My left and right shoulders were constantly being bumped by other guests.

By what means did they get that far up? For an instant I thought that question was in every glance cast upon me, then the next instant I thought it was only in my own head. Everything was smothered in collective joviality, as if a generous helping of sauce had been poured over it all so as to even out the taste. From here on it's just us. What we did to get here doesn't matter anymore. When all is said and done, we all took the same path. The path that leads here. To the feet of Power, Heavenly Light and Olympus!

A pair of watery eyes cast what I took to be a sour glance at me. Maybe my presence was an impediment to their enjoying the happiness they were about to savour. What's this mere mortal doing in a place set aside for the elect? So he filed a report, okay. So he denounced someone, all right. But it's far too soon to call him up here! If it weren't, then half the population of Albania . . .

But the nausea set off by those weepy eyes was soon dispelled. The brass band opposite the platform carried on, thumping out its rousing marches. The flags began to flutter a little more vigorously in the breeze, as if they knew it was nearly ten o'clock. I caught sight of Th. D. one more time, then lost him from sight. Maybe he was going on even farther. Perhaps up to stand B, or even to stand A . . .

8

The strange sensation of bewilderment persisted in my brain. It was probably euphoria induced by being so close to power. Flags and marching bands had a purpose, after all. They played their part.

My intoxication would surely have been complete if it hadn't been for the taste of a funeral in the back of my throat. Suzana's funeral. I had lost Suzana at the same time as I gained access to this stand. The flowers and the music and the august scarlet drapes would have been just as fitting to mark her passing. Her sacrifice . . .

> *O Father, hear me! she implored*
> *Young and innocent though she felt*
> *Her sobs and cries could not melt*
> *The stony hearts of men set on war*

What I'd been reading in recent days about the sacrifice of Agamemnon's daughter would not go out of my mind. The festive hubbub, the brass band and the watchwords written on the red banners didn't take my mind off the subject, they actually brought it back with greater intensity. Two thousand eight hundred years ago, a large crowd — just like this one, moving towards the grandstand — converged on an altar that was probably similarly draped in red.

Why are you all in such a hurry? — What's going on? — Didn't you know? — They say Agamemnon's daughter is going to be sacrificed —

A rumour to that effect had been going around troop-infested Aulis for some days. It was true that the wind hadn't stopped blowing, and the sea was still foaming around the ships anchored close to shore. But despite the weather, most people were puzzled when they heard the alleged reasons for the delay in setting out for Troy. Was it just the high wind, or was there something else? *We had our fill of wind coming over here, more than enough of it. If the leaders are at loggerheads over something, like I've heard said once or twice, why don't they come out and admit it?*

"Excuse me, Comrade, do you have the right time?"

I was so lost in my own thoughts that if the man who asked me the time had touched my elbow, as people sometimes do, I would surely have jumped like a jack-in-the-box. And that would have prompted God knows what suspicions!

I was aware that someone was smiling at me, and

I thought: Now you're really going out of your mind, you've forgotten who people are! Then I realised that the person in question was smiling at someone else, with a face as worn and as lined as a dried fig. I don't know what drew my attention to the person, whose skin was creased into a shape that could have been a smile expressing disbelief or irony or some other meaning unknown to mere mortals. It's Suzana's father's top adviser! I realised. When he was at a meeting we televised a year before, one of my colleagues had whispered into my ear: *That's Comrade X's right-hand man.*

I studied him with as much concentrated hostility as I could muster. Had he or had he not known in advance of Suzana's impending change of heart? He must have known, seeing as he was her father's closest confidant. Maybe it was even worse . . . Maybe he was the instigator of her sacrifice! Like Calchas . . .

My imagination flew off once again to the ancient seaport of Aulis. The rumbling swell and the ceaseless comings and goings of soldiers dotted all along the shore made the atmosphere of suspended activity almost palpable. Most of them were dreaming of giving up war and going back home to their wives or sweethearts. A rumour that the campaign was about to be cancelled gave them hope of just such a turn — but suddenly, like a bolt from the blue, came quite different news. In order to calm the winds, Agamemnon, the commander in chief, was going to sacrifice his own daughter!

Most of them didn't believe their ears. Supporters of the commander of the fleet didn't believe it because it saddened them too much. Was such a sacrifice really necessary? Agamemnon's opponents didn't believe it — they were reluctant to admit that the chief was capable of such self-denial. And people who were hoping for the straightforward cancellation of the campaign didn't want to believe it, either.

No, something like that just wasn't possible. It was utter madness; it was uncalled for. As for the wind, old seadogs confirmed that it wasn't so bad it required such a tragic step. Anyway, who could be sure it would make the wind abate? After all, it was that soothsayer Calchas who'd come up with the idea — and everyone knew how unreliable he was.

I scanned the crowd to find Suzana's father's adviser again, but I'd lost him. If I had managed to locate him, in the crazy mood I was in I might have been capable of approaching him and asking out loud: "So it was you, wasn't it, who gave Suzana's father that piece of perverse advice? But *why* did you do it? Go on, tell me why!"

Robert Graves's book dealt at length with the issue of Calchas. According to the oldest sources, his personality was as puzzling as could be. It was known that he was a Trojan, sent over by Priam with the specific task of sabotaging the Greeks' campaign. Eventually, though, he'd gone over to the other side, become a turncoat. So you couldn't avoid wondering whether he was a genuine renegade, or whether his new allegiance was just a strategic cover. It was equally possible, as often happens in circumstances of this kind, that after facing numerous dilemmas in the course of a war whose end was nowhere in sight, Calchas had ended up a double agent.

His proposal to sacrifice Agamemnon's daughter couldn't have been a key step in his career. (Let's not forget that his prophecies, like those of any turncoat, were treated with scepticism.) If he were still secretly in Priam's service, then obviously he would ask for the sacrifice of the commander's daughter, to foment further discord and resentment among the increasingly fractious Greeks. But if he'd genuinely gone over to the Greek side, the question would then arise whether he truly believed that the sacrifice would placate the winds (or whatever else: passions, disagreements), and thus permit the fleet to set out.

Whatever he was, a true or sham renegade, an *agent provocateur* or a double agent, his advice was just too wild, not to say lunatic. A soothsayer, especially in times such as these, must have had many enemies just waiting to use the tiniest of his blunders against him. So if he had made the suggestion to Agamemnon, he would have been sure to lose out in the end.

Far more plausible, therefore, was that Calchas never said anything of the kind, and that the idea of sacrifice had been invented by Agamemnon, for reasons known only to himself. He must have seen how easy it would be to implicate Calchas after the event, to justify his crime in the eyes of enlightened people and to mask its real motive. It was even quite possible that raging winds and so on hadn't even been mentioned as the fleet was preparing to depart, and that the sacrifice had been performed without a word of explanation . . .

The soldiers and civilians of Aulis had converged at the place where the altar had been set up. Maybe invitations had been issued, to prevent the place being overrun. Everyone in attendance must have been on the verge of asking the obvious question: *What is this sacrifice? What's it for?* The very absence of a clear answer would have heightened anxiety and fear tenfold.

No, Calchas hadn't given any advice at all. A prophecy from him would have seemed too dubious, too Machiavellian. But in that case, why had the idea of sacrifice sprung from Agamemnon's mind like an illumination?

Groups of spectators drifted like ripples lapping rhythmically on the shore towards the places with the best view of the parade, or towards the central stand where the top leaders would take their seats.

I was drifting imperceptibly myself with the same end in view when I saw Suzana. She was in C-2, a little lower down than I was, together with other sons and daughters of the elite.

She was subtly pale, and her indifference could be guessed partly from her profile, and partly from the glistening comb that held up her luxuriant hair. She was staring vacantly in the direction of the band.

Why are they asking for your sacrifice, Suzana? I questioned her silently, with quiet sorrow. What storm are you supposed to appease?

For a brief moment I felt entirely empty. Gripped by the sense of void and exhausted by so many questions, I wondered: Am I not going too far with all these analogies? Isn't it altogether simpler — a woman naturally pulling back from an affair when an official engagement is imminent? I was the victim of what was, after all, a quite ordinary change of heart. Was my mind not simply trying to give my defeat a tragic dimension that came only from its own nature?

I'd got hold of the word *sacrifice* and then used it to contrive an analogy I'd taken further than was warranted. I was no better than a novice poet who manages after much effort to spawn a metaphor, then falls for it entirely and constructs an entire poetic work on a foundation no more solid than sand.

I would never have thought that a sudden perception of a likeness between Suzana and Iphigenia — one of those random, instantaneous illuminations that flash across men's minds thousands of times every day — could take root in my mind and grow to the dimensions it had now acquired. The identification had become so complete for me that I wouldn't have batted an eyelash if I'd heard an announcer on radio, on TV, or in the theatre introduce "the daughter of Agamemnon, Suzana!" However, the equivalence was also what allowed me to see in an instant a whole new side of the ancient drama, in the light of the present situation of Suzana and her father. It made a new sense of the relations between Agamemnon and the other leaders, of their power struggles and fallback positions, their reasons of state, their use of exemplary punishments and of terror . . .

For a while, my mind seemed intent on casting off a too heavy burden, and made a concentrated effort to de-dramatise the whole thing. But all of a sudden the well-oiled machine in my head jammed, clashed gears, and went into reverse. A massive and fearless NO took hold of my entire being.

No, it couldn't be that simple! Sure, I was at the end of my tether, I was flailing, but all the same, I was utterly certain that things were not so simple. It wasn't so much the word *sacrifice* or Graves's book that had planted the seed of the analogy in my head. It was something else, something that I could not quite see for the fog surrounding it, but which I could feel quite near. It must be here, in full sight, all I had to do was to shake off a veil that was clouding my vision . . . Had not Stalin sacrificed his own son Yakov to . . . in order to . . . to be able to say that his own son . . . had to share the same destiny . . . the same fate . . . as any Russian soldier? And what had Agamemnon been trying to say two thousand eight hundred years ago? What was Suzana's father trying to get at now?

My thoughts were interrupted by the sight of her head, swaying between the shoulders of two others. I don't know why, but the memory of our first meeting suddenly came back to my mind. Portrait of a young girl bleeding . . . That's how it had crystallised in my memory . . . It was one afternoon late in the autumn. After our first kiss on the couch, she looked me in the eye at leisure, then said with quiet composure: I love you. She maintained her quizzical stare, as if checking to see that I'd understood her. She needed only a sign from me to offer proof of what she'd just said, and when I responded — rather hesitantly, as I was somewhat taken aback at the prospect of such an easy triumph — "How about lying down?" she got up right away and, with the same placid manner as she had spoken, got undressed.

I followed her orderly gestures. Her lace lingerie appeared when she took off her dress, and when she pulled down her tights her smooth white legs came into view. I got up from the couch and kissed her as cautiously as if she were sleepwalking, and pressed a bunch of her hair to my right cheek. *I like expen-*

sive women . . . I mumbled, without knowing then or since whether "expensive" referred to her Western underwear, to the valuable comb that embellished her hair, or to the ease and simplicity with which she offered herself.

On the couch she put up no resistance. She'd taken off the last of her underwear, and everything would have happened as perfectly as in a painted dreamscape if an abrupt, subterranean tremor hadn't suddenly shaken us apart. Her earlier eagerness gave way to opposite emotions of awkwardness and tension, which she tried but failed to hide.

"What's the matter, Suzana?" I asked, still trying to catch my breath.

She didn't answer. But I guessed that a kind of safety catch had clicked on somewhere right inside her and locked her up, and then I thought I understood. But I was greatly surprised nonetheless when she blurted out, point-blank: "I'm a virgin."

We lay for a long while on the couch without speaking. Then, with a smile that was more like a brightening above her cheekbones, she said to me: "That wasn't very nice, was it?"

I didn't know what to say, but she went on: "That's why I preferred not to tell you beforehand."

I felt unable to react, perhaps because happiness had shown itself in its most certain form, surrounded by a halo of sadness. The triumph, which a short while before had seemed to come so easily, now felt like a feat of arms. *I beg you, Suzana, don't be my downfall!* was my unspoken prayer.

9

The band suddenly stopped playing, the loudspeakers roared with a storm of applause, and all heads turned towards the central stand. The leaders were coming out onto the platform. From where I was sitting I could make out only some of them. I couldn't manage to see the Guide, or Suzana's father, who was maybe standing at his side. From the C-1 stand, only four of the leaders' heads were visible. Were they really over-sized? Maybe it was just the effect of the nickname that one of our colleagues in the music department was alleged to have given them — "the bigwigs". He'd been sentenced to hard labour in the mines for having asked why, after forty years of socialism, most of the members of the Politburo still had to come from the least educated layer of society. That's what he was sup-posed to have said at a dinner party. But some people claimed he'd gone even further and declared that the government of the nineteenth-century League of Prizren had been better educated than the one we had now! Well, that's what he was supposed to have said, but it wasn't even mentioned at the meeting where we voted to fire him. The same thing happened in my own case, presumably because it was thought too dangerous to say it out loud, even as incriminating evidence. So, again like the case I was involved in, he was found guilty of professional lapses, of having sloppy ideas about Western music, and of making sarcastic remarks about productive labour . . .

The New Man is the Party's greatest triumph . . . our most famous victory . . . the happiest land on earth . . . no debt, no taxes . . . the one and only Socialist nation!

I hardly listened to the dire and deadly opening speech. Those hopeless, irremediable clichés that we'd all heard a thousand times went in one ear and out the other, as such things usually did. Some of the current watchwords, like shadows cast by the hand of a master puppeteer, summoned up the shapes of the people they'd helped to bring down. You only had to open your eyes and look around to find slogans, symbols and portraits that had served directly to bring some people to ruin. For instance, the Constitution forbade any borrowing from foreign sources, any reference to the availability (that is to say, to our shortage) of butcher meat, and any allusions to the decadent Jean-Paul Sartre or to the shape of Mao Zedong's eyes.

Our colleague in the music department had been luckier than one of the technical controllers, however. That young man had taken a swipe at the privileges enjoyed by the elite and their offspring, such as villas and foreign travel. Once again, he wasn't openly blamed for what he'd said, but for different things, like his notions about free love (which were just about enough to get him thrown out of work). In the meantime, he was caught talking to a foreign tourist, and that really did him in. During his trial, and despite the plight he was in already, he stuck to his guns (so people said), denouncing "The Royal Court" as before, but laying it on thicker than ever, accusing the leadership of transferring gold and diamonds to foreign banks as if we were still living in the days of King Zog, of committing secret assassinations, and other equally sinister deeds. He hadn't spared a soul, not even the Guide, but he'd been specially harsh about his wife, whom he'd described as the true inspiration for her husband's crimes, a real Lady Macbeth — Lady Macbeth of the Backwater, he'd said, the Qiang Qing of Albania, and so forth. He was sent down for fifteen years, but he never served a quarter of his sentence. In the chrome ore mines, people said, there were deep pits, in whose vicinity common criminals frequently bumped into politicals, by accident. That's how it all ended: a gradual fall from grace, from season to season, from year to year, cruelly summarised in a headlong rush lasting a few seconds.

The privileges of the leadership and especially of their children was one of the regular topics of argument with my uncle. However, unlike all the other subjects we argued over, this particular argument did not send him into a frenzy. Though he would never admit it, he probably felt ill at ease with the privileges himself. My polemics with him on this subject stopped the day I met Suzana. She amazed me. Were the rumours about the children of the top rung just idle gossip, or was she different from the others? I quickly came to understand that the latter hypothesis was correct. Suzana was indeed different in every way.

That's why you've been singled out for sacrifice, I said to myself.

But in the moment of thinking that, another thought hit me unexpectedly, like a giant wave: what

if the sacrifice was only a show? What if Suzana's simplicity and modesty were only for appearance, whereas
in reality, over there behind the high walls of official
residences, villas and private beaches, she was having
a riot at all-night parties with unlimited booze and sex
on tap?

A pang of jealousy cut me to the quick. Hadn't I
read page after page on the possibility of Iphigenia's
sacrifice also being a sham? On her having been replaced on the altar by a fawn at the last moment? And
so on. A classic show designed to impress the popu-
lace. Typical leadership solution. My Suzana at shore-
side villas all winter long, dancing till she dropped,
then stripping naked and offering herself on a couch,
groaning with lust . . . No, no! Rather she were dead
and done with!

One afternoon I'd recorded her sighs and groans
on tape, and late at night, when everyone else was
asleep, I would shut myself in the kitchen of the apartment to listen to them. Hearing her voice dissociated
both from the act and from the sight of it made a
strange impression. The voice was even but porous,
full of breathing sounds and blanks. Street sounds —
a policeman's whistle, a distant car horn — added a
cosmic dimension, like shooting stars on a summer's

night streaking unpredictably at the edges of the boundless sky.

However many times I rewound the tape and played it over again, the sensation of cosmic void did not diminish but grew stronger. I felt I was far away, out of touch with her. At some moments, it was as if she were buried in the ground and I was listening to her complaining from the grave; at other times I was the one who was buried, but could still hear her moans through the clay soil and over the racket made by the upper world.

On one occasion I turned the volume up as high as it would go, as if I'd wanted her heavy breathing to fill the universe, and then I caught myself thinking that apart from her black pubic area I'd never had a decent look at her sexual organ, the true source of the raging storm.

When we next met, with the seriousness that was hers in all matters relating to love, she took up a position such that beneath her pubic hair I could see the pale pink lips of her sex. I studied them for several seconds, and I guess my eyes must have expressed the surprise of a man who hears something growling fiercely in the bushes and then suddenly sees through the foliage not a fearsome monster, but an inoffensive pet.

Suzana's sex looked utterly simple compared to its sophisticated function. In spite of myself I compared it to what my previous girlfriend's looked like. Her organ could have been called imposing and almost baroque, like a pleasure factory. But maybe it had not always been so, maybe it had become that way from use . . . So many ejaculations had gone down it! And not only mine. She — my other girlfriend — had had relations with two other men before me, and maybe that unspoken truth was what exaggerated the proportions in my eyes. But Suzana was only a beginner. Maybe later on, after all the pretenses to come, her sex would also become more complex. Later on, when I would have lost my rights . . .

10

A sudden burst of brass and drums made me jump. It was the start of the parade.

It was the same old routine we'd seen so many times on television. Gymnasts formed patterns with vaulting poles bedecked with bunting, bouquets and wreaths. Then colour-coded squads of boy and girl athletes. Next would be the factory delegations, steel-workers in the lead, as always, followed by miners, textile workers, shop assistants, cultural workers, then neighbourhood groups, then school parties, dum de dum . . . Jiggling stiffly up and down over all those heads came the outsized portraits of members of the Politburo. My gaze attached itself to one of them in particular, the portrait of Suzana's father. Why had he asked his daughter to make such changes in her dress and in the people she saw? What was the message? What was the symbol?

It would have been perfectly comprehensible if he'd taken that step out of fear, or if he suspected his foothold was giving way. But he wasn't on a downward trajectory. On the contrary, he seemed to be climbing by the day. And it was that rise, specifically, that had engendered the word *sacrifice* and had directed it to the remodelling of Suzana's future.

His portrait was now almost level with the grandstand. For the tenth time I exclaimed inwardly: What *is* the message?

Years before, the terrible campaign against cultural liberalisation had begun just that way, with a step so small as to be almost imperceptible. A letter came in from the province of Lushnjë casting aspersions on the dress worn by the presenter at the Broadcasting Service's Song Contest. Accompanied by sly grins and snide comments, the letter went on up from the music department to one of the assistant directors of the radio service. (*All right, the presenter's dress was a bit too long and caused offence. That's because those bumpkins are still living in the last century! They get everything wrong. You can't really hold it against them . . . unless this is a put-up job?*) In much the same state of mind, the assistant director, more out of curiosity than because he took the matter seriously, showed the letter to the Head of Radio. He was a naturally timid man, so he didn't laugh out loud, but he didn't make a big fuss about it either. He just said: "You must be careful with things like that, sometimes they can get you in deep shit," and that sobered up the assistant director on the spot. It was only when they were having coffee a couple of days later with the Head of Broadcasting himself — Big Boss, as we all called him — and the latter interrupted the guffaws going on all around to inquire about that "famous letter from Lushnjë" that the assistant director felt the weight off his shoulders.

So they had all had a good laugh over coffee together: the Head of Broadcasting, the Party secretary, and the quaking Head of Radio.

It wasn't long before the laughter stuck in their

throats. A week later Big Boss himself got a telephone
call from a branch of the Central Committee asking
about the letter. Why hadn't an answer been sent out?
The Head of Broadcasting protested vigorously: It
wasn't the job of the Broadcasting Service to follow
through on every piece of correspondence that came
in, especially one as stupid as that!

Everyone who heard about what happened, including subordinates who had no great love for Big
Boss and who would have been delighted to know
he'd received a rap on the knuckles, were for once all
agreed that he had been right, and that they'd all had
enough of letters from the grass roots.

A few days later, however, the Head of Broadcasting was summoned to a meeting of the Central
Committee, and he came back to the office with a
long face. A meeting was called the same afternoon.
The Party secretary reminded us of the attention we
should pay to comments coming from the masses, and
then read out his own self-criticism. The Head of
Broadcasting spoke next, briefly. After emphasising
how fatal it would be not to value the views of the
masses at their true worth, he too (and this was quite

unprecedented!) read out a self-criticism dealing prin-
cipally with the letter from Lushnjë.

All of us in the Broadcasting Service found that
was going too far. Right after the meeting and several
times over the following days we discussed whether it
was necessary for the dignity of the Head of Broadcasting to be tarnished for such a trifling matter. We
were all of like mind that it was not appropriate. It was
all the more inappropriate because Big Boss was himself a member of the Central Committee and on this
issue, after all, he had done no more than defend the
interests of the Broadcasting Service.

It has to be said, however, that apart from feeling
revolted by the affair, all of us (probably including Big
Boss himself) felt a degree of relief. Because it meant
that someone's yearning to take the Head of Broadcasting down a peg or two (which was the sense we
made of the whole manoeuvre) had now been satis-
fied. All it took were two or three well-chosen expressions, copied from the watchwords stenciled on walls
(*Always learn from the people! Keep things simple!* and so
on) to have the affair wrapped up. Self-criticism was a
truly miraculous cure.

It did not occur to any of us to think we might

have been wrong from start to finish. A week later, after the Party meeting where we were told that the boss and our other superiors had restated their self-criticisms, but with greater attentiveness and gravity, we got notice of a full staff meeting. *Can it be about the same old business? — I can't believe it! — Can you imagine, going over it all again, in front of everybody?*

The purpose of the meeting turned out to be exactly what we had surmised. A representative of the Central Committee was in attendance, and he threw his piercing glance at everyone in the room in turn.

"I have as it were the feeling that you've treated this business a little too lightly, Comrades. You thought a handful of superficial self-criticisms would do the trick and there was no need to dig into the causes and roots of evil. But the Party won't be hoodwinked as easily as that!"

Big Boss's eyes drooped with weariness. Weary, too, were the faces of us all. For it was but the start of a whole string of meetings that we would have to attend, like stations of the Cross. We would come out of it unrecognisable as our former selves, with our skin torn, our flesh bruised, and our bodies marked by it forever.

Our initial arguments about respect for the authority of the Head of Broadcasting, our fear of offending him, and so forth — how antiquated they now seemed! We were in a different climate, and our priority had to be to shelter from the hailstorm that was going to rain down on every one of us. Each new day brought utterly unexpected changes in mental composition. What was absurd, unimaginable, literally impossible on a Monday turned out to be quite alright on Tuesday, when it promptly began to eat away another, even more horrifying barrier.

The first to meet his comeuppance was the Head of Radio. He tried to defend himself by claiming that he had at least shown some anxiety about that letter from Lushnjë (which was true). Had he not said: "You must be careful with things like that, sometimes they can get you in deep shit"? But that was what sealed his fate.

"So why didn't you raise the issue, since you were anxious about it, eh? So as not to incur your boss's displeasure? Out of servility, hmm? Or worse? Speak up, Comrade! Ask yourself! You're much more dangerous than your scatterbrained colleagues. You see evil staring at you, and you turn a blind eye!"

After the Head of Radio had been banished, first to the countryside, then to the mines, most of us thought that, what with the scapegoat having been found, the hailstorm would abate. Nothing of the sort. Meetings continued to be called at the same gruelling frequency. The most awful part was realising we were getting used to the idea of what had seemed to be, only the day before, a sombre foreboding too ghastly to seem plausible. At the bottom of each hole, another hole opened up beneath us, and we all thought: Oh, no! Not further! There has to be a limit, things are already abominable enough! But by the next day the abominable had turned into the sort of thing that nobody found surprising anymore. What was even worse was that wavering minds strove to find a justification for it.

Each day we felt the cogs and wheels of collective guilt pushing us further down. We were obliged to take a stand, make accusations, and fling mud at people — at ourselves in the first place, then at everyone else. It was a truly diabolical mechanism, because once you've debased yourself, it's easy to sully everything around you. Every day, every hour that passed stripped more flesh from moral values. Minds became drunk on an unwholesome brew: the euphoria of self-debasement, of universal corruption. *Sell me, brother, I won't hold it against you, I've sold you so many times al-*

ready . . . And the noose of collective guilt carried on tightening around our necks.

At first sight, you might have said it was nothing more than a war machine set in motion by malice, ambition, and the thirst for revenge. But a closer look would have shown that things were more complex than that. Like an alloy composed of extremely varied materials, it contained utterly contradictory ingredients: cruelty as well as compassion, repentance alongside unbounded joy at not having been struck down — which itself gave way almost instantly to the superstitious fear of having to pay for such luck. The complete absence of coherence and logic only increased people's fatalism. Thus even those who had refrained from joining in the hysteria also got hit. They aroused a bizarre kind of commiseration that had the outward form of resentment. *Poor guys! But, from another point of view, it serves them right, they were too hasty in thinking they could get off lightly* . . . The hysterical were also taken down — those who had yelled louder than anyone else against the accused, and called for the heaviest sanctions. Their fall raised a wave of satisfaction. *Serves them right! Everything has to be paid for in this life* . . . And the blade also fell on those who dug in their heels and refused to write a self-criticism at first; but the pit was just as deep, if not deeper, for those who'd been in a hurry to confess their sins and to testify against themselves.

It was impossible to know what was the better course — to stay in your shell or to come out fighting; to be prominent or just one of the crowd; to be a Party member or outside all parties. As it is during an earthquake, people ran about in all directions looking for shelter, but buildings that looked solid and shock-proof would suddenly collapse. Everything was shifting, nothing remained still, and this profound instability affected thoughts and behaviours. Reasoning was put out of joint, whims of resisting vanished into thin air, as did any thought of revolt. Nobody would have dared ask what was going on or why. And you didn't feel angry in the slightest, just as you wouldn't think of railing against thunder and lightning.

Was the plan to scatter and destroy us all so that only the state would remain standing, like an inaccessible, untouchable Fate? Or was there just some mysterious set of circumstances allowing the storm to rage ever on? The force of its gale, the way it gusted from unexpected angles, and the sheer randomness of what it knocked down certainly incited terror. What was quite noticeable, however, was that it also aroused admiration for Power.

As we went from meeting to meeting, our mangled souls and diminished beings became ever more unhinged. A comrade of mine who worked for the courts told me that a similar kind of decline usually set in among prisoners held in solitary confinement, especially during the first phase of the investigation. We, of course, could go out into the open and mingle in noisy crowds, but we felt as isolated as if we had been incarcerated between the four walls of a cell. Maybe even more so.

By now the letter from Lushnjë had come to seem as remote and unlikely as the omen that in bygone days was believed to tell of a coming plague. Where was that letter now? On what shelf, in what archive had it been filed? In what wardrobe now hung that only slightly overlong dress that had provoked the fatal letter?

If anyone had said a few days ago — a whole era ago — that the letter that prompted the Head of Broadcasting's witticisms over coffee would one day cost him his job, we'd have split our sides laughing. But that day had come, and nobody found it surprising. We were all rather more inclined to feel a kind of relief. The boil had been lanced at long last! The cure would bring peace to all, and not least to the Head of Broadcasting himself. Granted, the penalty could hardly have been more humiliating for a member of the Central Committee. Big Boss was redeployed to manage municipal services in a small town called N. That's not too bad a deal for him when all is said and done, people opined. He would still have a car. All right, only an old banger. But a jalopy is still a car — and a whole lot better than being eaten away by anxiety.

Of course, you could look on the bright side. Yes, the hurricane had drifted away from the Broadcasting Service and was now battering all the other institutions of cultural life. It was said that grievous errors of liberal inspiration had spread their tentacles almost everywhere — to the Union of Writers and Artists, books and magazines, and film production . . .

11

The brass band's beat was now keeping time with the train of my thoughts. For a short while, I'd imagined the band had paused and then started up again even more deafeningly. Actually, there had been no interlude. It was just an impression, perhaps a consequence of taking in the music while lost in my mental re-enactment of events at the Broadcasting Service. I must have incorporated the music unconsciously and allowed the furious and sinister flourishes of drums and brass to mark time to the horrors of that past madness.

The hurricane had sucked up writers, ministers, allegedly right-deviationist ideas, movies, senior civil servants and plays. Amid the general chaos, the expression "rightist deviation in cultural affairs" often floated to the surface, and in its wake came the even more ominous phrase, "anti-Party group".

Compared to what was going on in the capital, the circumstances of the former Head of Broadcasting in the little town of N. — which most of us had first considered utterly degrading — looked idyllic. To be responsible only for house painters, toilet repairers, and swimming pool maintenance workers! That was an oasis of peace compared to areas in the eye of the storm, as Ideology and Art now were. Some people must surely have envied him in secret . . .

The peace didn't last long, however. One day a

delegate turned up at N. to attend a grass roots Party meeting for the locality that now provided the entire horizon of the former Head of Broadcasting's political landscape.

"In the light of recent events, what do you now have to say to the Party?"

The meeting at which he lost everything he still had — his membership of the Central Committee, his Party card, his job as manager of municipal services and his official car — was not a long one. Next morning he turned up for work as a municipal labourer wearing an old pair of dungarees and a paper hat of the sort house painters wear to protect their hair from splashes of whitewash, and maybe he thought he had touched bottom then. No one can say what he really felt, however, because from that day on nobody ever spoke to him. He worked alternate weeks as a house painter and as a tile layer in apartment bathrooms, a silent and nameless being under a paint-splotched cap.

In the end, if somewhat late in the day, peace, or the soggy kind of calm that buckets of whitewash, white ceramic tiles, and especially mute anonymity seem to induce, would probably have come to him. So he must have been truly shaken by the knocking on the door in the small hours when they came to arrest him one day. He was destined to know the fear of falling one more time, just when he thought he'd got to the bottom of the abyss and was safe from any further descent.

The question "why?" — the accursed question that had nagged at him ever since he had begun to fall, right down to the day when they put on the handcuffs — was finally about to get an answer.

But answer there was none. Indeed, during the investigation, as he lay all alone in his prison cell, he found it harder and harder to imagine what it might be. So it went on until the day he was charged and heard the heavy prison sentence pronounced: fifteen years.

After all that, he must surely have felt relief. The relief was certain now, nothing could threaten it anymore, and it tasted almost like bliss . . . because he could not possibly have known of that dark, deep and nameless pit in the chrome ore mines. And when in the half-light some unknown hand shoved him into it, he hardly had a moment to think about anything at all. The fall was so brief it left no time for questions, dilemmas or regrets. Maybe he left this world screaming, but it could only have been by instinct, like the futile attempts we all make to stop ourselves from falling by grasping at the sides of the well. But his desperate arm-flapping, that vague, instinctive reminiscence of bygone ages when birdmen still flew, remained unseen by any human eye. Maybe the very absence of witnesses was what gave his fall its unreal dimension, and made it like an echo of the ancient tale about falling to the netherworld.

But where could you find eagles to bring you back up? And supposing you did find a bird to carry you, all that would ever be seen of you again would be dry bones.

12

The band went on pounding out merry tunes. Squads of miners, whose plastic helmets made them look like dwarves, were now marching past the stands. Maybe they come from the chrome ore mines, I thought. I'd so often tried to wipe that story from my mind, but it kept coming back, like an obsession. I was certainly not the only person to have wondered hundreds, maybe thousands, of times if that notorious letter really had come from Lushnjë, or whether it had been penned somewhere else and then discreetly planted in one of the letter boxes you could find at street corners almost anywhere.

The purge of the army, which came soon after Culture had been dealt with, began in the same kind of way. It was generally thought that it had started with a tank manoeuvre carried out directly across from the offices of a neighbourhood Party committee. The purification campaign in the industrial sector, on the other hand, was set off by a handful of ore — ore with a suspicious gleam that betrayed an attempt at sabotage. Someone eventually managed to trace the lump of ore, which like the presenter's dress and the design of the military exercise, had led to a procession of coffins, right back to the Central Committee.

"Stop that!" I ordered myself, again and again. I did not want any more recollections, I wanted only to commune with my sorrow. But the same old thoughts kept buzzing around in my head. The dress, the exercise, the suspicious nugget . . . But what could have been glinting in it, if not a beam from the Beyond?

What had happened in our meeting room was rehearsed in the most varied walks of life and on a far grander scale, right across the nation. Soldiers who had treated the rout of the artists as a joke and rubbed their hands gleefully as they watched it unfold (*Serves those liberal guys right! They've had it too good for too long! It's their turn to take the rap!*) shook like reeds when they saw the storm rushing towards them. Later on, people in industry, who'd crowed about the military's foolish self-assurance, met the same fate. From then on, workers in other sectors kept their sarcastic comments to themselves as they waited anxiously for their turn to come.

Like successive bouts of the same disease, the now familiar attitudes recurred: people lost their tempers, then collapsed, then tried to justify why they had been lacking in courage, then they submitted and turned their backs on the victims. *No smoke without fire! Why else would they have been punished so harshly?* It got to the point where you couldn't find any Valium at the chemist (just asking for a box of tabs became a suspicious act). Couples split up, people had depressions and mental breakdowns.

It had all been laid out as if in a prophetic triptych entitled *Still Life with Long Dress, Military Map and Nugget of Ore*. But there was still room on the canvas — for Suzana . . .

I scanned the sea of shoulders until I found what

I was looking for. What sign of the zodiac do you represent, my darling, my dangerous love? I muttered.

Now, if that had all happened before the great purges, if it had occurred to someone in that long-gone age to think that a change in the way the daughter of a senior official dressed might signal a coming political storm, and if, as a result, he'd looked up books on classical mythology to find in them God knows what terrifying analogies, then that someone would have probably been treated as a madman, or else as a hysterical agitator throwing oil on the flames in order to make everyday life more dramatic than it really was.

But meanwhile the purification campaigns had happened for real. Even if they'd faded from memory, those campaigns, like great rivers leaving the trace of their passage wherever they flood, had left various layers of mud in us all. So it took just a hint, such as we'd not have noticed in times gone by, to strike fear into our hearts and minds. The merest sign would reawaken a *danse macabre* of slumbering ghosts, make us superstitiously alert to symbols, keep us forever on the lookout and bring back in turn suspiciousness, foreboding and ancient nightmares.

So it wasn't so much Graves's book or that Suzana's father was a prominent figure in the political leadership of the country nor any other such fortuitous similarity that had drawn my mind to construct an analogy with an ancient tragedy. The parallel came simply from the real events of a few years before, which were still clawing at us ferociously. Had these events never happened, then Suzana's declaration that she needed to change her way of life would have been no more than the conventional way in which a well-brought-up young woman displays the necessary moral correctness when an official engagement is planned.

A ripple and then a wave of whispers ran through the crowd on the stand. *What was that? What's going on?* It took a few moments before we heard that somewhere over on stand D or B, diplomats from Eastern bloc countries were taking their leave. The same thing happened every year as soon as the first placard excoriating the Warsaw Pact appeared. A few minutes later a beanstalk of a boy appeared holding up a placard declaring *The Theory of the Three Worlds Is a Reactionary Theory!* Now it was the turn of the Chinese delegation to make itself scarce.

Muted laughter swept across the stands.

Meanwhile, as the placards that had prompted the departure of the Eastern bloc representatives came level with our stand, my eyes were riveted in stupefaction on the other watchwords: *Live as in a State of Siege! Discipline, Military Preparedness and Productive Labour!*

From the corner of my eye I was watching the guests standing around me. Which one of them would have to leave the stand next? For it had surely already been worked out on which day, at which hour, each one of them would be ejected from the cohort of celebrants . . .

I turned towards stand D to try to catch a last glimpse of Th. D., as I reasoned that was where he must be. Had his hour now come? Or had it already passed without him noticing?

And what about you? I asked myself. You're playing at guessing when others might fall, but do you know how much time *you* have left?

A gleam from the comb in Suzana's hair drew my thoughts towards her once more. No, it definitely could not have been just a wish to maintain her image, or a passing bout of modesty in the run-up to the engagement or a piece of advice that the Supreme Guide might have dropped in her father's ear. *A little more discretion would be advisable, if only for a while. There's been too much gossip of late about what our youngsters are up to.* No, I could see more clearly than a Cassandra the coffins and the executioner's bloody axe hovering over the altar.

Stalin's portrait was making its way towards us now, swaying gently in time to the synchronised march of the placard bearers. Those eyes with their creases standing in for a silent smile filled the horizon. What about your son Yakov? Why did you sacrifice him . . . ?

I could not take my eyes off the huge painted banner bulging in the breeze. Your son Yakov, I kept on muttering, may he rest in peace . . .

I was surprised by the resurgence of that obsolete expression, for it had been completely expunged from the language taught to people of my generation. Dozens of similarly gentle and compassionate set phrases that reminded you of the precariousness of the human condition had likewise been erased from daily life. Just like belfries, prayers and candles; and alongside them, pity and repentance . . . Lord, they have eradicated everything so completely — so that nothing should be left standing to bar the way of crime!

Why, why did you make an offering of your son Yakov? May he rest in peace . . . Every day your field marshals tried to make you reverse the decision. There was nothing unusual about swapping prisoners of war. It would be even more straightforward in the case of your son. For one thing, it would be good for your own peace of mind. In the current circumstances, the fate of us all hangs on that. But you dug in your heels. *No, and no again!* What *was* in your mind, O Sphinx, when you said that?

Suzana's father's portrait was in something like tenth position, not far from Stalin's. You'll never understand the reason for the change in Suzana, he seemed to be saying to me. You may be able to get inside her vagina, even inside her heart, but you'll never know what she herself is unaware of.

The serried ranks of the procession stretched out into the far distance. The only thing missing was a portrait of Agamemnon. Of Comrade Agamemnon MacAtreus, member of the Politburo, grand master of all sacrificers after him. As the founder and classic example of his kind, he presumably knew better than anyone else how the springs and levers of this affair had been set.

13

The parade seemed to be about to come to a close. As tradition required, the tail of the procession was made up of representatives of our cultural institutions: the opera, the national ballet, the Kinestudio and Tirana University. I hid my face as best I could when my colleagues from Broadcasting Services came level with the stand. Then behind them came the technical controllers, the make-up people and the evening news presenters in long dresses, like vestal virgins . . .

It was all over in just a few minutes. As the last squads of activists yelled their last chorus of applause and moved off briskly toward Skanderbeg Square, the stands emptied faster than you would have thought possible. Invited guests climbed down from their seats with a slightly flummoxed look on their faces, as if they were coming away from a dinner party for which they'd had excessive expectations, or from a trial, or from a sexual encounter. I glimpsed Suzana a couple of times but then lost sight of her again.

Little by little I ended up back on the Grand Boulevard, in a slow-moving crowd, under a sun that now felt scorching. Cardboard wreaths and silk flowers were scattered over the pavement. Burst and trampled balloons lay in the dust. The giant effigies, which no one was now bothering to hold up straight, were leaning against walls and fences, staring at a slant, and sometimes upside down. There was a palpable sense of sweaty fatigue, of winding down, letting go.

Two thousand eight hundred years before, Greek soldiers had probably left the scene of Iphigenia's sacrifice in a similar state. Their faces had blanched at the sight of blood on the altar, and in their hearts they felt a gaping hole they didn't think would ever leave them. They said not a word, and in any case they had hardly anything to say, except for the same few thoughts that kept on going around in their heads. Private Teukr, for instance, who up to then had planned on deserting at the first opportunity, now felt as if that idea belonged to a vanished epoch. Idomene, his comrade in arms, who'd been determined to answer back if his commander should dare speak to him roughly, now found that idea quite foreign as well. Same thing for Astyanax, who'd been planning on sneaking off to see his fiancée, an idea that up to then had seemed easier and easier as his longing for her grew greater. Anything light or happy or likely to lessen the tension of war — joking, slacking off, going wild with loose women — was now dangerously close to being extinguished for good. If the supreme leader Agamemnon had sacrificed his own daughter, that meant that there would be no pity for anyone else either. The axe's blade was already smeared with blood . . .

I suddenly thought I could see the answer. The sensation of breakthrough was so strong that I stood still and closed my eyes, as if the sight of the external world might cloud what was at last coming clear . . . Yakov, may he rest in peace, had not been sacrificed so as to suffer the same fate as any other Russian soldier, as the dictator had claimed, but to give Stalin the right to demand the life of anyone else. Just as Iphigenia had given Agamemnon the right to unleash the hounds of war . . .

It had nothing to do with the belief that the sacrifice would calm the winds that were keeping the fleet in port, nothing to do with a moral principle declaring that all Russian young men were equal before death. No, it was nothing but a tyrant's cynical ploy.

I know what you're after, too, what you're trying to use Suzana for . . . You probably won't sully your blade with warm blood, but though you may keep it bright and clean, it won't be any the less harsh or brutal.

Perhaps I had sensed it long before, and had been approaching the truth step by step ever since Suzana told me of her decision. What her father had requested looked pretty insignificant, but it was much more than it seemed. Though hidden from the general gaze, it was a sacrifice to be counted among the cruellest ever invented. The letter from Lushnjë, the suspicious lump of ore, or that fatal military map, had led to lines of coffins, but Suzana's sacrifice would certainly have consequences even bleaker than those horrors . . . Should untold thousands of cancelled evenings out count for less than a heap of corpses? Or poisoned Novembers, evening conversations choked as by an odourless gas, and the snows and smells of winter all sullied and soured? Blue benches around the swimming pool turned into useless accessories, student parties gone as flat as stale beer, tangos without a beat, bronze clocks striking midnight in empty hallways, hair brushed in front of the mirror, and jewels, and furs and make-up gone all streaky and worn . . .

Yes, Suzana was the harbinger of an irreversible impoverishment of ordinary life. A life that like a cactus in an arid desert had barely managed to accumulate a few last drops of human vitality.

You were nothing but a poison and the spectre of the scourge! I exclaimed in my mind. Your change of heart was really the continuation of the campaigns sparked off by the letter from Lushnjë, the ore and the map. There was no Calchas whispering advice; no, Suzana's father probably didn't even know why he was acting as he did. Someone else, the Supreme Guide, who was in the process of appointing him as his official successor, must have asked him to do it. "Papa's as tenderhearted as they come," Suzana had confided, "he's completely incapable of scolding me."

Maybe the Guide had also grasped the man's real character and found a way of saying: Choose one of the two axe blades. If you aren't up to using the bloodstained one, use the clean one instead. But while I'm still alive, show me what you can do, and show me now! Strike! If you know how to use it properly, the clean blade can be the more fearsome of the two.

So what Suzana portended was the clean blade. Worn out by the rampage of the bloody blade, the country was now going to suffer a different kind of terror.

My God, spare this country from dehumanisation! I screamed silently. Protect it from yet another ruination! For it is about to inflict on itself what the sweaty haze and desert dust of the East has failed to achieve!

The placards of the now weary activists could be seen swaying as they moved off in all directions. *Revolutionise Life Ever More! Learning, Labour, and Military Training!*

But I've been staring at it throughout the parade! I thought. Those were the watchwords that had been repeated over and over these past few years. Those were the values that were supposed to replace lovers' sighs at sunset, melancholy moments on the verandah, jewels and dance bands. Productive labour, military training, studying the works of the Guide . . . But as they'd not yet stamped out all normal life, a new campaign was being set in motion.

Let us work, live and think revolution . . . Let us revolutionise everything . . . How many years of such a drought would it take to reduce life to a stony waste? And why? Only because when life is withered and stunted, it is also easier to control.

I had a pounding headache and remained incapable of controlling my train of thought. How the hell can you revolutionise a woman's sex? That's where you'd have to start if you were going to tackle the basics — you had to start with the source of life. You would have to correct its appearance, the black triangle above it, and the glistening line of the labia . . . Re-educate it by abolishing all trace of its past: all memory of orgasm, all recollection of thousands of years of pleasure . . .

I would have burst out laughing if I hadn't felt so dismayed.

The revolutionary triad: learning, productive labour and military training . . . And what would become of the dark delta of a woman's sex? A parched, desiccated estuary dotted about with puny blades of yellowing desert grass.

I'd never seen such a dense accumulation of placards. Ah, here's the notorious one about grass: *We shall eat grass if we have to but we will never renounce the principles of Marxism-Leninism!*

"You blind fool!" I said to myself. "The truth was right there, in front of your eyes, but you tried to find clues by going back three thousand years! You combed through books and racked your brains to find something that needed no research at all."

"So what?" I responded to my self-accusation. "Was I wrong? The signal that Suzana gave me was clear and precise, and that was the main thing. Whereas murdered Iphigenia wasn't around to testify for the defence. On the contrary."

Everything was happening as it had happened before, but in a perhaps even crueller way. Greek ships are leaving the coast of Aulis for Troy. One by one they haul up their anchors, spilling clumps of mud and stones into the choppy waters. The mooring lines are being cut, like last hopes.

The Trojan War has begun.

Nothing now stands in the way of the final shrivelling of our lives.

Tirana, 1985

The Blinding Order

1

By the last week of September it became obvious that the sequence of events could not have been just a string of coincidences. No sooner had he sung his first call to prayers — and done so admirably, in the view of all who were lucky enough to hear him — our new young *hodja* Ibrahim fell down the minaret stair. Next, we learned that the crown prince had been taken ill, likewise after a public appearance. Two or three more unusual things then happened in a row before the end of a week which had a real twist in its tail. As he was making his way to the imperial palace, where he was widely expected to make the long-awaited announcement of his government's agreement to a substantial loan, the British ambassador was involved in an accident, and his carriage overturned.

Bystanders chased down the alleys in pursuit of someone — a woman, or perhaps a man wearing a veil — who had stared at the landau as it crossed Blue Mosque Bridge a few moments before toppling over, but in vain, which is why the culprit was never found. But everyone agreed about one thing: the ambassador's accident, the young *hodja*'s fall and the sickness of the crown prince, as well as other facts of a similar kind, must have had a single, common cause. It was the evil eye.

This was obviously not the first time the eye had exercised its maleficent power. Collective memory, not to mention the archives and annals of the state, were full of similar occurrences, which tended to prove that from time to time, when aroused, the eye could spread misfortunes and calamities on an epidemic scale, if not worse. So there was no reason to be surprised that since time immemorial people had often had recourse to the saying: "He's been struck by the evil eye!"

Maybe because of the cold wet weather that autumn, or because of the economic crisis, the harmful actions of the carriers of the evil eye were doing more damage than ever. That made people all the more tense and angry, just as it provided unusually detailed material for the report that, people said, had already been submitted to the sovereign.

The sultan's response had been expected for days. If it was not to be a decree (some people were convinced it would take that form), then at least there would be a decision, or a proclamation, or perhaps a secret circular.

By Tuesday evening, no edict had been issued by the imperial chancery. And as always in such circumstances, initial speculation about the expected measures were embroidered by yet more badly muddled tongue-wagging.

In times gone by, any suspected sabotage by an "evil eye" was punished by harsh measures of the same order as those meted out to heretics: the guilty were thrown into a pit of quicklime, flayed alive, or stoned to death. People in the capital still remembered the flaying of Shanisha, an old woman who with a single stare had managed to transmit the *haut mal* to the daughter of Sultan Aziz's predecessor, which caused, first of all, untold sadness, then the latter's long illness, and finally his deposition, itself followed by far-reaching disturbances from which the state took years to recover.

That was how carriers of the evil eye used to be dealt with. But in the modernised, reformed state of today, this kind of punishment looked barbaric and out of date.

So what was the right thing to do? Should carriers

of the evil eye be treated kindly, and allowed to in-
dulge their practices to their hearts' content, until
they bring down not just men, but the very walls of
our houses? People opposed to clemency for carriers of
destructive glances, and those who stood more generally against any relaxation of the laws of the state,
were asking these questions. As a matter of fact, do
you know of a single case, they would ask, where evil
has been stamped out without a firm hand? Were you
thinking of obliging the carriers of the evil eye to put
on those glass things invented in the land of the
giaours,* those diabolical lenses they called *spectacles*?
Or would you rather cover their eyes with a black scarf
to make them look like pirates?

No, such measures would be pointless, they said.
The evil eye projects its poison just as — or maybe
even more — effectively through a blindfold, and obviously more powerfully through those accursed glass
things, even if you blacken them with soot, as fashionable young men in the capital had recently started
doing.

Such were the comments of the people who were
trying to determine what measures lay in store, up to

*Christians

the very day — a Friday — when, at long last, the decree was issued.

Like all great edicts, its title was very short: *qorrfirman*, meaning, literally, *blind decree*. However, it was neither as harsh nor as merciful as might have been expected. It was a decision that cut both ways, leaving the opposing parties equally unsatisfied, but in a muted way, which allowed their veneration of the state and its sovereign to assert itself nonetheless — especially with respect to the sultan, who showed himself once again able to rise and to remain above the mere turmoil of human passions.

With astonishing speed — within a week of promulgation — various details emerged about the cabinet debate that had given birth to the order. As was its wont, the Köprülü clan, which stood against the faction of Sheikh ul-Islam, had come out in favour of greater clemency in the treatment of carriers of the evil eye. The Köprülüs proposed to expel them from all state-sponsored activities, or else put them under house arrest, or, for the most heinous cases, deport them and concentrate them in isolated locations, as if they were lepers. On the other side, Sheikh ul-Islam and his followers supported traditional sanctions. The sultan listened to each faction and then decided not to favour either; or rather, he took both sides at once. The *qorrfirman* was such a canny concession to both clans that it channelled resentment of the opponents of barbaric sentences against Sheikh ul-Islam, just as it directed the fanatics' feeling of disappointment toward the Köprülü clan. The sultan had kept himself above the squabble, and he had not just earned the admiration of both sides but also provoked a special emotion tinged with sorrow at seeing him obliged to intervene in the interminable quarrelling of the clans, despite his more pressing preoccupations.

News of the order's main provisions spread among certain circles in the city even before the text had been read out by public criers or printed in newspapers. The main thrust of the *qorrfirman* was as follows:

> Cases of affliction by the evil eye having recently increased, and with the risk of *misophthalmia* (the original term, *sykeqoja*,* was dug out of some ancient dictionary) turning into a real scourge, the state, acting in its own interests and those of its citizens, has felt obliged to take a number of measures.

*Eye trouble

Carriers of the evil eye would no longer be sentenced to death, as they were in the past; they would only be prevented from perpetrating any more of their wicked deeds. That aim would be achieved by depriving them of the tool of their crimes — that is to say, of their evil eyes.

So the *qorrfirman* stated that anyone convicted of possessing maleficent ocular powers would forfeit his or her eyes.

People affected by this measure would receive compensation from the state, with a higher sum going to afflicted individuals who turned themselves in to the authorities. *Disoculation* (the first time the term had been used in an official document), that is to say, the forcible putting out of eyes, would be inflicted without compensation upon all persons who opposed the Blinding Order by whatever means, or tried to hide from it or to escape its application.

The call went out to all subjects of the age-old Empire to denounce either openly or anonymously any individual who possessed the power. They should put at the foot of their letters the full name and exact address or place of work of the accused. Denunciations could be made of persons of all kinds, be they ordinary citizens or civil servants, whatever their rank in the hierarchy of the state. That last sentence left many people gazing dreamily into space, as if they'd just been staring at an invisible speck on the far horizon.

2

Shortly after the introduction of newspapers, it became readily apparent that some kinds of government announcements were more effectively disseminated by the traditional channels of communication, namely town criers, whereas others had much more impact through the medium of print. This variation was of course related to the nature of the announcement and whether its audience was to be found primarily among the illiterate masses or among the elite.

Whether spread by ear or by eye, however, the *qorrfirman* aroused instant horror. But it could only be grasped fully if ear and eye worked together to transmit its meaning to the brain. Perhaps that was the reason why people who first heard it proclaimed by a town crier rushed to buy the newspaper in order to read it, while people who first learned of it in the press left their papers on café tables or public benches to hasten to the nearest square to await the crier's arrival.

An old feeling, which people had perhaps forgotten

about in recent years, suddenly began to seep back into the atmosphere. The feeling was fear. But this time it was no ordinary fear, like being afraid of sickness, robbery, ghosts or death. No, what had returned was an ice-cold, impersonal and baffling emotion called fear of the state. Bearing as it were a great emptiness in its heart, the fear of the state found its way into every recess of the mind. In the course of a few hours, days at most, hundreds of thousands of people would be caught up in its cogs and wheels. Something similar had happened six years previously, when there had been a campaign against forbidden sects (the latter had nonetheless managed to re-emerge since then). An even earlier precedent came from fifteen years before, when they'd unravelled a huge plot, which at first appeared to involve only a narrow circle of high officials but which came by stages to wreak its horror on many thousands of households.

People's natural inclination to erase collective misfortunes from memory made them forget — or believe they had forgotten — the peculiar atmosphere that arises just prior to a major outbreak of terror. Between the first hint of the threat and the first blow struck, in the time when the hope that the horror will not truly come, that evil might be thwarted and the nightmare extinguished, people are suspended in a state of paralysis, deafness and blankness that, far from placating terror, only serves to aggravate it.

They thought they had forgotten, but as soon as the drums rolled and the criers bawled out the first words of the Blinding Order, they realised they hadn't forgotten a thing, that it had stayed inside them all the while, carefully hidden like poison in the hollowed-out cavity of a ring. As in times past, before their minds had quite caught up with what was really going on, their mouths went dry and gave them a foretaste of what was to come.

It was clear from the start that what was now being put into place would be even more abominable than the campaign against forbidden sects and all previous episodes of the sort. That was because the new campaign's target was something so abstract it could never be quite pinned down. All the same, everyone grasped the impact it was bound to have. Even when the axe had been supposed to fall only on specific circles, as in the case of the campaign against the sects, or on isolated officials, as in the affair of the anti-state conspiracy, everyone, and all their relatives too, had felt its effect. This time, though, given that the issue related to something as manifestly indefinable as the maleficent or beneficent quality of a person's glance, and insofar as said quality pertained to something as universal as eyes (everybody had eyes, nobody could claim exemption on grounds of not being concerned), this time people were sure that the new campaign would be of unprecedented scope and violence. It was obvious that the vicious whirlwind would flush out every single suspect and whisk every last one of them off, without mercy, to their fatal punishment.

In homes, offices and cafés, people spoke of nothing else from early Saturday morning. But just the way things had happened during previous campaigns, this time, too, people talked about the Blinding Order in a manner completely at odds with the dark foreboding that it aroused in their souls. They treated it in an offhand, almost entertaining way. Apparently, people thought that as far as their personal relations were concerned, lightheartedness was the best way to ward off the least suspicion that might have lurked in their own hearts or in others' that the order might be directed against them as individuals in any way whatsoever. All the same, in the midst of conversations and laughter, a moment would come when eyes would meet and glances freeze into razor-sharp shards of ice. It was the fatal moment when each speaker tried to fathom his interlocutor's mind: Does he really think I have *that kind* of eyes?

These tense interludes would last barely two or three seconds. One speaker or the other would relax his stare, and then laughter and chatter would resume with even greater jollity. The discussions mostly focused on the same issue, an issue most people pretended not to take to heart on their own account. Just what *were* evil eyes? Was there a reliable way of identifying them?

There was a wide variety of opinion on the matter. People referred to the traditional view that the evil eye was to be found typically among light-coloured irises and rather less among darker hues, but everyone was also aware that eye colour was not itself a sufficient means of diagnosing *misophthalmia*, especially as the problem arose in a multinational empire where some ethnic groups had eyes — as well as hair and skin — that were more or less dark than others. No, hue was certainly not an adequate criterion, it was just one factor among many others, like squints, or the unusually large or small size of the eyeballs, which could similarly not be considered determining factors. There could be no doubt about it: no single trait, nor any particular combination of them in an individual pair of eyes, offered definite proof of the presence of *misophthalmia*. No, it was something else, something different . . . A peculiar combination of the intrinsic nature of the eye and of the trace its glance left in surrounding space . . . Of course, it was rather hard to detect, especially because the order mentioned no specific sign that might be of use in the matter. But if the order itself did not stoop to such minutiae, the special commissions that had been set up in more or less every locality must obviously have been given instructions and precise directions in order to identify this maleficent force and to ward off erroneous interpretations and possible abuses.

At that point in the conversation, people usually stifled an anxious sigh and turned back to lively, lighthearted topics.

That's how it was in office chatter, in cafés infested with informers, or even in homes when visitors were present. But when people found themselves alone, they would rush to wherever they could find a mirror and stand there for minutes on end. People with dark eyes tried to convince themselves that their pupils were sufficiently dark to clear them of all suspicion. People with light-coloured eyes tried to convince themselves of the opposite. But the people who stared longest at the mirror were those with squints, or eyes reddened by an allergy, or by high blood pressure, or by some other ocular irritation, as well as people with eyes bleary from jaundice, bloated from toothache or drink, down to people who suffered from a cataract.

Apart from those who were already blind, nobody could be quite sure he was exempt from the order. As everyone soon realised, that was the source of the *qorrfirman*'s mortal power.

Although some people told themselves they could keep the evil at bay by putting on a happy face and joking about the matter at every opportunity, others began to withdraw quietly from public life in the hope they would be forgotten. They shut themselves up at home, often staying in bed with their heads under the blanket, as they made mental lists of their personal enemies, or of all the people who envied them their jobs in the civil service and who might take advantage of the situation to make some critical remark about them. Among the latter, some tried to get ahead of the game by denouncing their enemies first, hoping that even if they didn't manage to destroy them in time, they would at least undermine the force of denunciations yet to come.

Meanwhile, as rumours and gossip about the new

order reached their peak, steps were no doubt already being taken, admittedly behind a veil of secrecy: the first denunciations must have been made, and the first lists of suspects based on those denunciations must have been in the process of being compiled. A central commission had now been set up and entrusted with the task of directing the campaign. It was provided with myriad branches in every province of the empire. Shortly thereafter, strange new locales sprang up under a name even more bizarre, composed of the Ottoman term *qorr* prefixed to a word borrowed for God knows what reason from the cursed language of the *giaours*: the new bureaus were called *qorroffices*.

People gathered in knots in front of the freshly painted signboards and even though the word *qorroffice* was most often glossed underneath as "Blinding Bureau" in smaller lettering and in parentheses, passersby almost always asked: "What are these *offices*? And what are they for?"

What were they for? That was only too obvious! Are you living on the moon? Didn't you hear about the latest order handed down by our great sultan, may Allah grant him long life . . .

Even so, the precise function of the *qorroffices* was not made clear right away. Some thought their only function would be to collect denunciations and to pass them on to higher authority; but others — who grasped the fact as soon as they saw deliveries of high-sided cots equipped with straps on their side bars, reminiscent of the gurneys used in hospital operating theatres — easily guessed that the *qorroffices* would be the very places where eyes would be put out. But in due course, especially at the height of the campaign, the nature of the *qorroffices* and their true purpose were made entirely plain. Apart from the fact that the offices collected the denunciations, which every subject of the empire could deliver by hand (even though the address of the central commission was widely publicised), these locales were all equipped with an official iron blinding bed, called the *qorryatak*. However, this piece of equipment was mostly symbolic. In practice the act of blinding was most often carried out elsewhere, except when it turned out to offer an opportunity to teach this or that area or neighbourhood or street a much-needed lesson.

As could be verified over the following weeks, the *qorroffices* were used less for collecting denunciations or for putting out eyes than for something quite different, throughout the entire campaign. Contrary to initial impressions, these locales, though as sinister and desolate as their name implied, became noisy and excitable gathering-places. People went there to find out how the campaign was proceeding, to get information on various details of the order or on the latest instructions from the central commission, to swap news about so-and-so who, after much shilly-shallying, had finally decided to turn himself in to have his eyes put out while singing the sovereign's praises, and so on.

Some people actually enjoyed spending part of their time in the *qorroffices*. They even brought along the cup of coffee they'd picked up from the corner café to drink it there; others, mostly youngsters, played messenger, taking away letters and coming back with envelopes or instruction sheets issued by God knows who; and there were even some who indulged themselves in speechifying, describing in sonorous tones and with a strange light in their eyes all the benefits that would flow from the *qorrfirman*, as a result of which the world, finally cleansed of the evil eye and saved from the dreadful effect of its evil power, would be a finer, more splendid place.

The almost festive atmosphere in the *qorroffices* was occasionally interrupted by the sudden entrance of a group of panting, cursing men dragging a carrier of the evil eye who had been caught in the act, or some other poor fellow convicted of having slighted the royal order.

However, despite the fact that the *qorroffices* had lost their sinister appearance and become more like public places, everyone agreed that it would not be at all easy to implement the Blinding Order. The central commission had issued a directive listing five acceptable ways of putting out eyes: the Byzantino-Venetian method (an iron bar forking into two sharpened tips); the Tibetan method (which involved piling heavy stones on the convict's chest until his eyes popped out of their sockets); the local method (using acid); the Romano-Carthaginian method (sudden exposure to a bright light); and the European method (protracted incarceration in total darkness).

The same directive also stipulated that people who turned themselves in, as well as some others who for various reasons were judged by the commission to deserve the privilege, would not only receive the regular monetary compensation but would have the right to choose the method of their own blinding.

It was easy to guess the two methods that would be chosen most often, and, moreover, be considered a signal favour by their victims, as being the Romano-Carthaginian and the European. Apart from the fact that they were painless, both methods left the victim's eyes untouched, resulting in no empty sockets or mutilation of the face.

The only difference between them was the length of the procedure. Whereas only two or three minutes of forced exposure to the sun was needed to blind the victim in the first case, in the second it required as much as three months of blindfolding for the sudden withdrawal of the wrap to provoke instant and total blindness.

The Romano-Carthaginian method, quite apart from the fact that it did not involve any psychological torture (long months spent in total darkness with depressing memories weighing down on you, and so forth), was carried out in conditions of blistering cleanliness, since it was based on the action of sunlight. As a result it rapidly became the preferred method among volunteers, as among other suspects, often from the higher social classes, who had no special protection from the *qorrfirman*'s wrath.

As for the other techniques based on force, compounding physical pain with mutilation and the lack of financial compensation, it was hard to say which was the most repulsive. The difficulty of choosing among them was, as people later explained, the reason for the hesitation often observed among victims, who dallied until, in the end, they asked their executioners to choose, begging them to bring their suffering to an end as quickly as they could.

With the promulgation of the instructions on the five different blinding techniques came other emergency measures that clearly indicated full implementation of the Blinding Order was imminent. The Medical High School launched an accelerated training programme in ophthalmectomy, several iron yards in the capital completed their first batches of forked iron bars for the Byzantino-Venetian style of blinding and other workshops began the manufacture of acid, which was stored in small and sturdy kegs intended to make sure it would survive lengthy transportation to the remotest provinces of the Empire. But nothing special was needed for the Tibetan method. Large stones could be found anywhere, and no particular preparation was called for.

3

Marie concentrated on finishing the domestic chores she shared with her sister-in-law, then, saying she had a migraine, went up to her room. Her sister-in-law scowled. They were both very young (there was barely a year between them), and they were in the habit of sitting down to gossip after the housework was done each day, until Marie's mother came to put a stop to their girlish chatter. "She worries that I might be telling you the secrets of my married life!" Marie's sister-in-law used to say with a muffled giggle. Marie, for her part, bit her lip.

She had heard a few of the secrets, actually, especially the day before her engagement was made official, and then more in the course of the following few weeks. Her eyes blazed with curiosity as she drank in her sister-in-law's sparse words, constrained by modesty and good manners to a mere trickle — whereas she thirsted for a raging torrent, as if she were lost in a desert.

But just recently, to the great surprise of her sister-in-law, who was inclined to be more open about things as Marie's wedding day drew near, the young woman had stopped asking about intimate matters.

The sister-in-law shrugged. What could you expect from a family of lunatics whose different members followed different religions?

She had been genuinely surprised when she found out that the family of her future husband, like many households of Albanian descent, had maintained over the generations the custom of including within its bosom members of different, that is to say opposite, faiths. Her father-in-law, Aleks Ura, was a Christian, but one of his sons, who had gone into the navy, had been brought up a Muslim; whereas the other, her future husband, remained a Christian. Maybe the father would have done the same with daughters had he had two of them, but since Marie was the only one, he had tried, in a sense, to split her in two. As he could not raise her in two different faiths at the same time (though such cases were not unheard of), he had given her two first names, each from a different religion. So for her first family and close friends, her name was Marie; for the rest of the world, including her fiancé, it was Miriam.

Her future husband had tried to explain to her the reasons for such duplication, which had to do with the fate and history of their far-off homeland, Albania, but she did not really get much out of his knotty explanations. All that was plain in her eyes was that the brothers of Aleks had followed two different faiths, and that their forebears and ancestors had always done the same.

In the course of the several weeks, during which

preliminary discussions relating to her engagement were held, she had been astonished at her own family's determination to become allied to this strange tribe, but it was not long before she learned the truth. The house she was going to join was related — distantly, it is true, but related nonetheless — to the famous Köprülü clan. To the degree that its name, Ura, was none other than the former and original patronymic of the Quprilis — translated, for reasons of state, from Albanian into the Ottoman Köprülü.

In fact, since her marriage she had not seen so much as a twig of the famous family tree, except for a nephew, a pasty-faced boy of ten or twelve, who had come to visit with his mother about a year ago. The boy was named Mark-Alem. He didn't say much, and when her father-in-law Aleks, who was eager to try to explain the origin of the family's name to the boy, had drawn a sketch of a three-arched bridge for him — a bridge located somewhere in central Albania where some kind of sacrifice had occurred in the dim and distant past — the lad just shook his head obstinately, and muttered: "I don't want to hear those gruesome tales."

A madhouse! the young woman thought once more, as her eyes wandered towards the staircase

Marie had taken on the way up to her room. What in heaven's name could she be doing up there on her own for hours on end?

She was not accustomed to spying on others, but after a brief inner struggle curiosity overcame her scruples, and she tiptoed silently to the top of the stairs. Once on the landing, she took a deep breath, looked around to make sure no one else was nearby, then crouched down and looked through the keyhole of Marie's bedroom door.

What she managed to glimpse left her dumb-founded. Marie was standing stark naked in front of the dressing mirror, putting on and taking off a pair of lace-edged silk panties.

Already? How can that be? the young married woman wondered, unable to take her eyes off Marie as she shifted her marble-white body from one slinky pose to another. For a second her crotch displayed its troubling black triangle before the silk swallowed it afresh.

No, she thought, as her mouth went dry, heaven only knows why. A woman cannot make movements of that kind unless she has experienced love. But was it conceivable that such was already the case?

Apparently the young wife must have made the

floorboards creak because Marie swung round suddenly and put a hand over her breasts. But she soon relaxed, probably because she saw that the door was bolted on the inside.

Her sister-in-law slowly withdrew and, with muffled steps, went back down the stairs as silently as she had gone up. They must have already slept together, she thought. That was also the only way of accounting for the lack of curiosity Marie had been showing recently.

She could not get that unbearably smooth white body out of her mind. The curvaceous hips that swayed at the slightest movement troubled her, and she thought to herself once again: Yes, yes, that must be it. There's no other explanation.

4

She was right. Two weeks earlier, something had happened quite suddenly between Marie and her fiancé which, to her mind, should not have occurred until their wedding night.

It was true that the family, like many others who had come down from the Balkan Peninsula, was relatively easy-going, at least in comparison to Muslim families in the capital. But however relaxed their behaviour and however eccentric the paterfamilias, no one within that family would have dreamed that Marie had spent time alone in a bedroom with her fiancé. And they could simply not have imagined she might have lost her virginity prematurely.

The day it happened had been no ordinary day, however. The new edict plunged everyone in the house into something like an inner maelstrom. From the nearby square came the roll of drums, then the voice of the town crier, declaiming the text of the *qorrfirman*. Marie had been unable to take her eyes off her father's face. It had turned quite livid.

She quietly went up to him and, as was her habit, placed a gentle hand on his shoulder, asking him sweetly: "What's worrying you so, Father dear? There isn't anything like that in our family, is there?"

Aleks shook his shoulders as if to cast off a cloak of weariness.

"No, of course not . . . Of course there isn't, my child."

She looked at her father with a quizzical expression, which repeated the same question in silence. He pretended not to notice, though it's possible that in the kind of trance he had fallen into he really didn't register his daughter's glance.

"And besides, the Köprülüs are distant cousins of ours, aren't they?"

"What?" the father almost shouted. "Cousins of the Köprülüs? Yes, sure we are, but in these kinds of circumstances that is of no use whatsoever."

Gradually his eyes narrowed, grew smaller, and at the same time his voice fell almost to a whisper. "In these kinds of circumstances it's better to have no cousins at all!"

At that moment there was a knock at the door. In came Xheladin, Marie's fiancé. His demeanour, unlike everyone else's, was so placid that Aleks glanced at him sternly as if to say, "Are you living on the moon? Haven't you heard about the *qorrfirman* yet?"

Very soon, even before the table had been set, they were all to learn the reason for Xheladin's seren-ity, or rather, his contained satisfaction. (He wasn't in a state of elation, of course, but set against their own quaking fear his quiet ease made him appear almost joyous.) Very soon they all heard what lay behind the future son-in-law's state of mind. Not only was he ap-prised of the decree, he knew rather more about it than any of them, for the simple reason that he had been summoned by his bosses two days before, and had been told he had been appointed a member of the central commission entrusted with the implementation of the *qorrfirman*.

Xheladin's words precipitated a sudden change in the domestic atmosphere. There was a sense of relief, accompanied by admiration for a future son-in-law who had been given such a demanding job. But that wasn't the main thing. The overriding emotion came from thinking — even if only vaguely for the time being — that as they now had their own man inside the citadel, at the heart of the machine, in the very lair of evil, then said evil would automatically be directed elsewhere.

Outright admiration could be read not only in the eyes of Marie but in those of her mother, her sister-in-law, and even her brother, who up till then had stayed aloof, heaven knows why, from his sister's fiancé.

Glad to have brought about a new mood, Xheladin relaxed and warmed up. An irresistible wave of good humour swept over the dinner table. The distant roll of the crier's drum now seemed to come from another planet.

Aleks's face was the only one that clouded over

from time to time, as if darkened by a passing shadow. He stared at Xheladin as if he were trying to make out what was going on in the depths of his being, under his skin, down in the marrow of his bones. And it was just when he had given him a stare of that kind that he put his hand on the younger man's arm and said: "I hope that when you're there you'll manage to keep clean . . ."

"What was that?" Xheladin said, imperceptibly drawing his hand away. "What did you mean to say?"

His face had suddenly turned icy and alert.

"Nothing, nothing," Aleks said with a smile, patting the young man on the shoulder. "Nothing, my boy. Maybe we'll talk about it again some other time."

Aleks was visibly sorry to have said what he had said, and for the remainder of the meal you could see he was trying to make up for his blunder. Merriness returned, and maybe it was precisely because people were not paying attention amid the good cheer that Marie and her fiancé, instead of going out on the verandah, where they were granted the right of whispering sweet nothings in private, quietly went up the stairs leading to the girl's bedroom.

Had the witnesses really not noticed, or did they only pretend not to have seen? Who knows? Maybe the mother and the sister-in-law really didn't see it, since they were busy clearing the table. The brother, who was barely able to stand, had already gone up to his bedroom. As for the father . . . he had probably not seen them doing it, unless — and this was the most plausible hypothesis, after those days of anxiety, and especially because he did not want to get snapped at after the recent incident at the dinner table — unless he had turned a blind eye and pretended not to see them. In any case, weren't they going to be husband and wife in six weeks' time?

The town crier's drum kept on rolling in the distance, giving as it were a new note to all life's ups and downs . . . Against this background noise, Marie put up no resistance to her fiancé's kisses, then she let him undress her and take possession of her as lord and master of the palpitating centre of her being. It all happened in complete silence, when in a brief instant pain and searing pleasure fought for ascendancy, each yielding to the other in turn. But unlike what her sister-in-law had told her, she didn't find the pain unbearable. Whereas the pleasure seemed to her without bounds.

A week later, when it all happened again (they had agreed he would come in without attracting attention, taking advantage of the fact that her parents had to go to a funeral), there was no pain at all, and the pleasure reached an intensity beyond words.

That was how Marie had come to believe she had nothing more to learn from her sister-in-law about the secrets of married life. She waited with feverish impatience for her fiancé to come, but this last week the only two times he had been able to visit (his work for that terrible commission was taking up all his time), they had not had an opportunity to be alone. So she waited for Sunday, when he would come for lunch as was his custom now, knowing intuitively that the miracle would occur once again. She and her sister-in-law had dealt with the morning housework, but whereas the latter expected they would then sit back in a corner and chat for a while, Marie, who wanted to take refuge in her bedroom to prepare herself for impending joy, said she had some kind of a migraine and went upstairs on her own.

She walked up and down for a while, then stood to look at the street along which her fiancé would presumably come, then her eyes lighted on the chest containing her wedding trousseau. In it, among scores of pieces of clothing, bed linen, and embroidery that had been collected over the years, lay a dozen pieces of underwear made of silk as ethereal as smoke trapped in a glass . . . Good heavens, why had she not thought before of giving him that surprise?

Previously, the sight of her sister-in-law's undergarments hanging out to dry over the stove had stirred awkward feelings and made her eyes cloud over. It had happened for the first time when she discovered the elementary secrets of married life. Such flimsy, delicate lingerie — the closest witnesses to the act of love and the fiery embrace of two bodies — seemed to her to be laden with mystery. They seemed especially charged in comparison to her own cold and lifeless undergarments, all neatly folded at the bottom of the trunk, as if entombed, still waiting to be brought to life . . .

She walked slowly towards the trunk, opened it, gazed at its contents, and began to go through the perfectly ordered and pristine pieces. There they lay, virginal and cold . . . Yes, she was going to try on every one of these diaphanous garments, each in turn, and she would baptise them, sanctify them, impregnate them with the warmth and the smell and the stains and the juices and the groans of love.

She quickly disrobed and, flushed with excitement,

began trying them on in front of the mirror. She wanted to choose the very finest for that day. The sky-blue pair? No, that other off-white one would be better. She had broad thighs, and when she made a slightly awkward movement her pudenda showed through. Marie sat on the kilim in front of the mirror with her legs slightly apart. Under the silk the lips of her vulva were half-revealed and she swallowed the saliva that raging desire brought to her mouth. Disconnected thoughts that seemed to come from outside raced through her mind. So that was the way into her body . . . Its porch ought to be pretty. She would decorate it with almond-flower lace, just as people decorated their thresholds with pots of flowering plants . . . Had her sister-in-law not told her that she had heard that women's sexual organs were as different from each other as their faces? Marie was sure hers was beautiful, and if it was, then why should he refrain from looking at it?

She got up; she took off one pair of panties to try on another, and then she heard a creak. She turned around in terror, but the door was well bolted, and she immediately calmed down.

She tried on most of her underwear, but came

back in the end to the off-white pair. She put them on, then slipped on her dress, and then sat down on the shaggy blanket on the divan, lost in thought. Each time she moved, the silk transmitted a soft, rustling reminder of its presence.

She did her best to banish the thought that was uppermost in her mind, but she realised that it was beyond her. She was henceforth entirely conscious of the fact that if she did not find a way of coming upstairs with her fiancé after lunch, the torture would be unbearable.

5

On Sundays lunch was served at the big oval table in the main room of the house. Xheladin arrived a few minutes after twelve dressed in a Western suit — a fashion that a good number of young men in the capital had recently taken up.

"How's it going?" Aleks Ura inquired when everyone had sat down at table.

The future son-in-law replied with an inscrutable smile.

"Fine . . . really fine."

They exchanged disjointed remarks about this and that. It took quite a while for them to get down to the issue they had all been waiting impatiently to hear about for the whole past week, that is to say, the *qorrfirman*.

"Are you getting a lot of denunciations?" Aleks's son Gjon asked.

Gjon was as fair as his sister, but when he got angry the colour of his hair seemed to darken.

Xheladin spread his hands wide in a gesture of explanation.

"How should I say . . . Yes, quite a few."

"And by what means is it to be established whether so-and-so really does have eyes possessing that power?" Gjon pursued.

Xheladin smiled. "We'll manage, one way or another."

"I have to admit that I think that will prove very difficult, if not impossible."

"It all depends," his future brother-in-law replied. "For instance . . ."

"For instance," Gjon cut in, "somebody, for entirely personal reasons, may find another's eyes to be evil, whereas someone else sees them differently. How are you going to deal with cases of that kind?"

Xheladin kept on smiling as he listened to his future brother-in-law, but his semi-scowl now seemed to be coming loose from his face, like a mask.

"You're right," he said. "However, to cope with such an eventuality, the central commission and all its dependent branches will abide by instructions laid out in an internal circular that defines in detail all the characteristics an evil eye must have to be counted as such. And contrary to what some people claim, external appearance is not the only criterion to be taken into account."

He gave a loud laugh and then went on: "I myself, for example, have fair eyes. According to those people, I ought to be a suspect and not even go near the doors of the central commission. And certainly not have a seat on it!"

Most of those at the table nodded. Since the day the *qorrfirman* had been issued, everyone had examined, directly or indirectly, the tiniest details of the particular characteristics of the eyes of the people they knew, and none among them needed to raise their heads from their plates to verify that Xheladin did indeed have fair eyes speckled with grey, which not only made them more charming, but gave his gaze a firm, cold and masculine air.

"No, external appearance is not the only thing. Such details have to be matched with others . . . I'm sorry, I know I am among my own kin at this table, but in the work that we do there are some secrets we are strictly forbidden to mention . . . What I can say, in short, is that before declaring that this or that person has the evil eye, we have to study and check every aspect of the case very carefully, and, when necessary, we go so far as to put the suspect under discreet surveillance for a time."

"Discreet surveillance? Well, well, that's something new," the brother said.

"Really?" Aleks's wife blurted out.

Xheladin nodded.

"All the same," Gjon continued, "I can't bring myself to believe that there really is a reliable, or, properly speaking, a scientific way of determining misophthalmia."

Xheladin said nothing. An angel passed, and the clicking of knives on bone china made the silence seem even more frozen. Aleks Ura shot a look of disapproval at his son, to no effect.

"I think that is precisely where the real power of the *qorrfirman* resides," Gjon went on.

"Where exactly is that?" his future brother-in-law asked.

Gjon did not reply right away. Perhaps in order to escape his father's glance, he cast his eyes up, over the heads of the seated guests, towards the French windows that looked onto the verandah.

"There's not the slightest doubt that the *qorrfirman* has given our people a seismic shock, and that it's disturbed them more than any other decree ever issued in our state," he said at last. "To come back to what I was saying, I think its fearsome power comes directly from the fact it's so vague. The Blinding Order makes each of us suspect our neighbour. Nobody is exempt from worry, we all feel more or less guilty. The power of the order derives exclusively from the all-pervading anxiety it induces."

"For my part, I think the power of any major edict derives solely from the sense of justice with which it is imbued," Xheladin said, sounding not irritated, but on the contrary, rather conciliatory.

At the end of this exchange, everyone felt relieved and breathed a little more easily.

"Is it true anonymous letters have been sent and that suspicion even hovers about the person of Grand

Vizier Muhta Pasha?" Gjon's wife cut in, maybe only to move the conversation onto a different terrain.

Xheladin shrugged. "I don't know," he replied. "That may be just gossip."

"Last year, there was another rumour of that kind, about Vizier Basri," Gjon said. "At first it was discounted as mere gossip, but then it turned out to be true, and the vizier ended up with a rope around his neck."

"Such things happen," Aleks Ura declared, determined to ensure that this time no hasty or ill-judged comments would be made at his table.

He had always been in favour of a less rigid adherence to rules, and sneered at people who did not allow women to join in the conversation; more generally, he did not hide his hostility towards the fanatical customs of the Asiatics; but even so, there had to be limits. Gjon's provocations had started it off, but now his wife was trying to pick a fight with their future son-in-law!

Xheladin's answers grew ever sterner, and he would probably have begun to show annoyance if he hadn't felt Marie's soothing glance on him from time to time.

Aleks hadn't missed the gleam of desire in his

daughter's eyes. They glinted in a different way than in the earliest days of her engagement, when she hadn't even tried to hide the attraction she felt for her betrothed. It was also different from the look she had in the following period, when her glance was, so to speak, denser. But now it was something else altogether. There was something so evanescent, fragile and vulnerable in her eyes that Aleks chose to avoid them altogether, for fear that an encounter might result in a painful clash.

Two weeks earlier, after lunch, at the same hour as now, he thought he'd heard them going upstairs to his daughter's bedroom. He was stunned for a moment, but then refrained from turning to look, like a man trying not to see a ghost . . . The wedding day was not far off, and the marriage seemed to him more and more like a really good idea. At times of worry, he felt an increasing desire to huddle with his nearest and dearest around the hearth, inside his own four walls, safe from the winds of anguish howling outside. What's more, his future son-in-law's new position gave them a precious source of news from the very heart of the mystery, just at the time when, as people grew more and more curious, it was becoming increasingly dangerous to say anything . . . His son and his rather scatterbrained young wife weren't able to appreciate this advantage; all they did was irritate their guest. But he, Aleks, was going to bring some discipline back to his too liberal table. He was going to bring it back right now, by taking sole charge of the conversation.

"Will the Order be implemented soon?"

He could not believe his own ears. How could he have spoken such words? He'd been working himself up to say something quite different, to move on to some entertaining irrelevance, so as to clear the atmosphere once and for all, and now his own mouth had gone and uttered other words, against his own will. You're getting senile, he thought. You've lost control of your tongue. Worse than a woman!

"Implementation?" Xheladin repeated. "Yes, I believe it will happen quite soon. Even very soon," he added after a pause. "It might even start this week."

"Really?" two or three voices squeaked.

"Is it true that distinctions will be made between the people singled out, as far as the means of putting out their eyes is concerned?" Gjon's wife asked. "Apparently things will be done differently, depending on whether the person belongs to the upper classes or not."

"That would be only proper, in this respect as in all others."

"I've heard talk of ways of blinding by exposure to sunlight. It's the first time I've heard of anything like that. Must be a new technique, right?"

Aleks Ura was about to butt in, but to his surprise his future son-in-law began to laugh out loud.

"No, the technique isn't new at all. On the contrary, it's perhaps the oldest of them all!"

So he began to describe empty beaches and villas and luxurious seaside hotels where those sentenced would quietly drag out as long as possible their last days of sight. One morning, when the sky was even clearer than usual, they'd be put in seats facing the sun, and there, in a matter of a few minutes . . .

"Neat work, you can't deny it," Gjon said. "No blood, no branding iron, none of those barbaric devices . . ."

"Well, I think it's the cruellest way of doing it," Gjon's wife said. "To be basking in the light of the sky and the sea, and then to be suddenly deprived of both!"

"Would you prefer the opposite means, being blindfolded and locked in a cell for three months?" Gjon asked.

"I think it might be less painful overall," she replied. "It would give you time to get used to darkness."

"I don't agree!" Gjon protested. "It must be dreadful torture. It must feel like your head is bursting apart with all the thoughts going around in it."

"For heaven's sake, could you please put a stop to this nonsense!" the mistress of the house broke in. "Can't you talk about something happier?"

She put the cake tray in the middle of the table and gestured to all to serve themselves.

"People say all sorts of things," Gjon said pensively. "Some people say that this whole story about the evil eye is just balderdash and that the people who cooked it up don't even believe in it themselves."

"What was that, young man? Are you sure you have all your wits about you?" Aleks interjected.

"I'm not saying that, Father," Gjon replied. "It's just what I've heard other people say. In their view, this whole thing is a set-up designed to keep people's minds off our economic problems."

"Enough of that!" Aleks cut him off. "I will not allow you to say such things!"

"But Father, I'm not saying that, it's only . . ."

"Listening to such opinions is itself a guilty act!" Aleks shouted, his voice shaking with emotion.

Meanwhile, Xheladin hadn't batted an eyelash.

6

The drums started beating again before dawn on Friday, this time to signal that the Blinding Order was about to be put into effect.

From behind their closed shutters and barred windows, with their hair still uncombed and their eyes puffy from having been suddenly dragged from sleep, people strained to make out the town crier's words. What's he saying? What's he saying? people whispered to each other. Keep quiet so I can hear! I think he's reading out names, lots of names . . .

By the next day the full roster of names of the first cohort of volunteers was made known. Directly beneath banner headlines reporting the start of the implementation of the *qorrfirman*, newspapers listed the last names of those who had initially volunteered for the *qorroffices*, together with the details of the cash bonus and annuity that had been granted each of them.

Several papers published the words of a certain Abdurrahim, a palace servant from the capital, who had declared: "I'm sacrificing my eyes very gladly. Apart from the satisfaction I feel at being able to do something that is useful to the state, I am grateful to the *qorrfirman* for having freed me from the awful pangs of conscience I felt at the thought that my eyes might be a cause of further misfortune."

Apart from the list of the original volunteers, the media provided scarcely any information about the overall number of people concerned, their whereabouts or the manner of their disoculation (this new term having entirely displaced the word *blinding* in journalists' prose in the space of a few days).

Some said there were hundreds of victims, others upped the stakes by claiming there were thousands, and that they were being kept in huge camps.

Meanwhile, amid all the efforts to clothe the campaign in festive garb, the hunt for evil eyes went on, openly or in secret. People who had up to then escaped the crowd's scrutiny were being denounced. Others who had been unmasked and gone underground were being ferreted out. Some who had heard or imagined they had been denounced had also gone into hiding, but because they were tormented by persecution mania their own behaviour aroused suspicions that soon led them to ruin.

The next Tuesday, the town criers were out again, summoning carriers of the evil eye to report directly to the nearest *qorroffice*, seeing that they could only benefit from taking the initiative. "The Prophet declared that being born with an evil eye is not a sin in itself!" they bawled. "Guilty is only he who hides that power!"

Newspaper columnists began writing stories about events connected with misophthalmia. A man by the name of Selim had been caught in the act in a thicket of bushes, staring with his evil eye at a bridge under construction and trying to make its arch collapse. The bricklayers enlisted passersby to help deal with the man. They'd chained him up and blinded him on the spot. The paper didn't state which technique had been used, but it was supposed that it was one of the three methods henceforth classified as the "harshest", unless of course the bricklayers themselves had thought up something entirely different and even more atrocious.

Stories about the *qorrfirman* in the papers were sporadic, but in the *qorroffices* there was never the slightest let-up. Volunteer messengers came and went bearing notes, new orders and instructions, and scarcely did they get to their destinations than they were off again, their faces beaming, or else gravely composed in order to express the full dignity of their function.

The hunt for the evil eye was now at its peak. *Qorroffices* competed against each other for results. When things were not going too well in a bureau of that kind, glum-faced workers, slaving away late at night by the light of oil lamps, would suddenly panic and pass each other names of people who lived on their block or street and who maybe had eyes of that kind, but who'd escaped notice up till then.

Sometimes lights in the *qorroffices* were on late into the night, and people who lived nearby, unable to get to sleep until the lights went out, muttered to one another: What the hell are they doing so late in the night? What new miseries are they cooking up now? May God make them stark, raving mad!

Meanwhile, threats against people who spoke ill of the glorious *qorrfirman* continued to be made — which didn't stop anyone from cursing it with ever greater vigour. People threw insults at it, and twisted its name this way and that, calling it the Dark Decree, or the Sinister Sentence, or the Fateful *Firman*. The same thing happened as far as gossip was concerned. Efforts to put a stop to rumours only made more of them flourish. They got weirder by the day, and some of them made your blood run cold. Just recently, for instance, a rumour about the grand vizier had made the rounds. Suspicion of the evil eye was said to have fallen on him, despite his being the sovereign's right hand. An anonymous letter writer had had the audacity to name his name. People could not stop talking about that piece of news, with a terror whose special flavour came from a combination of fear, curiosity and a kind of relief and contentment. *So there you are! Higher-ups can get in just the same mess as little folk!* But how could people question the grand vizier himself? . . . Why are you so surprised? As if this was the first time that kind of thing had happened . . . There's more to it, you know. It's said that the whole hullabaloo over the evil eye is really aimed solely at getting rid of the grand vizier! Look, I'm sorry, but what you've just said is completely illogical; if that really had been what the sovereign was after, if he'd wanted to topple the grand vizier, who in the world could have stopped him? There's no shortage of grand viziers who've gone to sleep one night with their heads on their shoulders, and found them cut off in the morning . . . Sure, sure, things used to be done that way, but times have changed. Nowadays they don't only use knives to deal with matters of state. It also takes a bit of skill. And besides, you're forgetting that the grand vizier was appointed with the heavy backing of the Köprülü clan. I guess you know you can't joke with that crew. To bring one of their men down, you'd have to lay the ground carefully, inside and outside the empire. Because people are talking about this overseas as well, you know . . .

Thus did gossip spread. But these particular rumours were not the only ones that were considered punishable. Attempts were made to root out things considered just as harmful, such as inappropriate witticisms, ironic remarks and anecdotes, alongside a number of puns and riddles.

One Saturday afternoon, the famous poet Tahsin Kurtoglu was summoned to one of the *qorroffices* in the centre of town. In front of a large crowd, and after it was first explained that a favour was being done to him, as a great poet, by having him summoned to a *qorroffice* and not to a court of law, he was asked to explain some lines of poetry he had published a couple of weeks before, as well as remarks he was said to have made here and there among his circle of friends.

As far as his poems were concerned (the issue revolved mainly around one of them, *We were struck by the bow not by the arrow*), the writer defended himself energetically, maintaining that it was but a simple love poem addressed to a woman graced with fine eyebrows, and the fact that he had declared the lady's brows (*the bow*) to be more fearsome than her glance (*the arrows*) in his lines of verse had absolutely nothing to with any kind of subversion of the glorious Blinding Order.

His listeners, visibly sceptical, then quoted back to the poet some of his double entendres, which he denied ever having uttered. Then someone in the crowd took a sheet of paper out of his briefcase and took it upon himself to read its contents aloud:

> On the seventh day of this month, during a dinner with friends, you declared that this great blinding would only deepen the darkness of the world. On the twelfth, in a café, you claimed there was a balance between light and dark, between the visible and the invisible, and that this balance between the two sides would now be broken, to the disadvantage of the light and the visible. And you also claimed — and this is the most heinous claim it is possible

to make — that the sum of the eyes of all human beings on earth, about a thousand million, make up what you called the eye of all humanity, and that it grows weaker when a large number of individuals go blind, especially when — and now you all listen to this! — especially when those blinded are the most clear-sighted of all!

After each of the sentences spoken by the *qorroffice* employee, Tahsin Kurtoglu shook his head, and when his accuser had finished, exclaimed: "Those are nothing but calumnies and fabrications bruited about by my rivals!"

These words, far from calming the crowd that had gathered, only served to excite it, and things began to get noisy and rough. People were even heard to shout: "You've let him have his say, now give him what he deserves, the Tibetan method!" "We want the Tibetan! We want the Tibetan!" others began to chant, but one of the officials, after signalling to the crowd to stop shouting, made a short speech in which he stressed the clemency of the state, which, on this occasion, would only reprimand Kortoglu. "But the main thing," he said, wagging his finger at the poet, "is that this is your last warning!"

Everybody could now see clearly that the tide of denunciations and poison-pen letters had gone over the top, and when people caught sight of the mail-wagon going down the street, they would stop to gaze at it in horror, as they knew that at least half its load consisted of just such kinds of missives.

It was on one of those gloomy days that Marie closed her bedroom door behind her, went to the window, and watched her fiancé go out into the street. He'd seemed altered, and rather sterner than usual. During lunch, despite her father's efforts to liven things up, the conversation had hardly got off the ground.

It was because of him, she could see it now! She watched him saunter down the street until he vanished behind the shade trees on the pavement, and the same thought occurred to her: he must be worried about something.

She ran through a list of possible reasons. Over-work, office intrigues, pangs of conscience . . . but in the end she began to wonder whether she had only imagined it. Didn't everyone sometimes wake up in a bad mood, which only gets worse when someone else remarks, "You don't seem your usual self today." That must be it. No doubt about it.

Only half-dressed, she went to the mirror and looked at herself, bending first one knee, then the other. There, at the top of her right thigh, she saw two bluish bruises, the trace of the preceding Sunday afternoons. Whereas the latest bruises would not become visible for two or three days . . . She looked for a moment at her smooth belly and the low black tufts that covered her crotch, then she sat on the carpet with legs half-crossed, and studied her sexual organ.

"It's all quiet now," she thought, "as if nothing had ever happened."

She could not take her eyes off the slightly curved line separating the pink lips of her vulva. They looked like lips that would never speak . . . And yet, just a few moments before, they had been almost crazily talkative, dribbling . . .

"Unbelievable," she said inwardly. It then occurred to her that a woman's sex was without any doubt the most inexplicable and enigmatic thing in the world. Those silent labia would never tell anyone what had gone on inside and around them.

Feeling suddenly grateful, she stroked her belly,

her crotch, then the lips themselves. But she soon felt
a shiver of cold, and got up to put on some clothes.

There's no doubt about it, something is worrying
him, she thought as she pinned up her hair.

7

The anti-misophthalmic campaign was now at its
peak. It rose higher every day like a rain-swollen
stream, sucking countless human lives into its headlong rush.

Evil eyes were not the only ones to be ceaselessly
hunted down. The same energy was devoted simultaneously to rooting out declared or supposed defenders of the evil eye, as well as individuals considered
to be covert opponents of the implementation of the
qorrfirman and the close and distant relatives and re-
tainers of owners of the evil eye. Other people were
charged with lacking clear sight, with indifference, or
with insufficient zeal. Sometimes, these latter folk
were able to make the same charges against their ac-
cusers.

An unprecedented disorder struck the vast state
like a hurricane. People now talked openly about
settling scores and power struggles between political

factions. Other voices proclaimed sentences against the very people who seemed best shielded from the storm — the functionaries whose job it was to put the *qorrfirman* into effect. The "bad-eyes", as they called them, had managed to infiltrate the *qorroffices* and even the central commission, and once inside, had exploited their positions to spread havoc.

"Aha," you could hear people muttering, "so that's why we thought, and on occasions even allowed ourselves to remark, that there is something strange about all this! Yes, it's an incontrovertible fact that only the sovereign is just. If you serve him devotedly, then you get your proper reward; but if you stray into error, if you commit a fault, however brilliant you may have been in your career of service up to that point, you will be punished like anyone else."

"You are right. We're so lucky to have him, may Allah grant him long life! Without him life would be a snakepit. Did you hear what went on yesterday in front of Tabir Sarrail?"

And that is how, despite all the turmoil and havoc, the most incredible stories managed to circulate. Now and then, like a straw borne on the crest of a wave, you got just a glimpse of that rumour about the grand vizier.

8

Everyone in the house must have noticed he'd grown slimmer, but she was the only one to mention it to him.

"You've lost weight," she said, after they'd bolted the bedroom door behind them. "Why? Is it from all the work you have to do?"

"Yes, I do have lots of work." After a pause, he repeated, "Lots."

"Come, you're going to forget all about it . . ."

She had now lost all modesty. She lay on the bed and first put her arms round him, and then her long, slim legs, of a white so pure that they gleamed in the half-light. She let out a faint, steady moan, which only at particular moments rose to a scream close to sobbing.

Moments later, when they were lying in peace, he cast his eye on the bluish marks on her naked thigh, where they looked like official seals. She expected him to make some comment about them, but to her great surprise the question he asked was of an entirely different nature.

"Have you ever approached the Köprülüs to ask them for help?"

She shrugged her shoulders in a gesture of surprise. "Why?"

"Oh, no reason . . . I just noticed that in your household you hardly ever talk about them."

"That's true. They really are cousins of ours, but only very distant ones. And anyway, my father, with his funny character . . ."

"I see," he said, not taking his eyes off the bruises.

She ran her fingers over his chest.

"You seem worried," she said in a caressing tone.

He averted his eyes.

"No, I'm all right."

"Does your work weigh on your mind?"

He shook his head. "Not at all. I have no reason . . . On the contrary."

"What do you mean by 'on the contrary'?"

"Stop asking me such irritating questions!"

"If that's how you feel!" she exclaimed, clearly annoyed. She tried to turn her back to him, but he held on to the sheet she was attempting to pull over her belly. A special, almost abnormal light in her fiancé's eye dissipated the squabble almost instantly, and she began to look at his face with great attention. His eyes were fixed on her crotch as if this was the first time he had seen it.

"In three weeks' time we'll be married, and we'll be able to stay like this for hours on end."

"Yes . . . Maybe I'll be given the leave I'm due at that time."

"Really? That would be wonderful . . . We'll get up late, and stay awake half the night . . . It'll be splendid to do it again when we're half asleep, in the middle of the night, in the dark."

He shuddered as if he'd just awakened from a daydream. "In the middle of the night, in the dark?" he almost shouted.

"Shh! Keep your voice down. What's come over you?"

"In the middle of the night, in the dark . . ." he said again, his voice now fading.

Slowly, she stroked his neck and his forehead. "Something is tormenting you," she whispered as if she were talking to someone asleep. "But don't worry. Basically, all you are doing is applying the law. Leave the remorse to the people who sowed this whirlwind . . . Do you hear what I'm saying? They're the ones who should have pangs of conscience . . . Now come here and do it again, my darling."

9

Eventually they heard that the grand vizier had been fired. Gossips first said he'd been relieved of the top job to take up a less prominent position; then they said he'd simply been asked to resign; finally, "asked to" was replaced by "told to". So it wasn't a demotion or a change of position, or a discharge for slackness in implementing state decrees, among them, in particular, the *qorrfirman*. No, he was simply being sacked, accompanied by house arrest, on the specific and savage grounds that he was afflicted with the evil eye.

Now, all the grand vizier's intimates and colleagues knew full well that their master had a slightly menacing cast. What surprised people was that the Sultan, whose eagle eye missed nothing, hadn't noticed long before.

"That's not so easy," others objected. "We all know now that crossed eyes aren't always evil, as long as they're not combined with other specific features."

"Yeah, yeah," people retorted, "those are things you can interpret any way you like."

Straight after the grand vizier's fall, the original rumour arose with new vigour: "Didn't we tell you that the ultimate purpose of the whole massacre was simply to liquidate the grand vizier?"

"Well, if that's true," came the response, "then tell us why, now that the purpose has been met, the campaign hasn't been brought to an end?"

"For the very reason of camouflaging why it was organised in the first place. Anyway, just as the terror machine takes some time to start up and to get into top gear, so it takes time for the brakes to bring it to a stop."

And just as it takes time for the dust to settle after a landslide, so it took quite a while for this shock and all the disturbance it caused to come to a final conclusion. A wave of purges, which everyone suspected would be the last, swept over the state. People had only one thing on their minds: keep clear of this rolling wave, for though it was most likely the last, it seemed well set to be the most murderous.

10

They were lying down together. She was entirely naked and he was half-undressed. He'd told her the truth only a few moments before. She hadn't screamed, hadn't sobbed, almost as if she'd been expecting the confession. She listened to what he had to say with her face as white as a sheet. Only when she nestled up to him did he feel her wet tears on his own cheek. That's probably the way the acid will trickle down over my cheekbones, he thought, after it has burned out my eyes. If his request to be blinded by the medieval European method (that is to say, by darkness) was rejected (he hadn't dared ask for the Romano-Carthaginian technique), then he would probably be let off with the acid. There is worse, an office colleague had remonstrated. Just think of the Byzantine, not to mention the Tibetan, which is the most awful by far.

"So when you told me you were going to ask for leave for after our wedding, you already knew?" she asked.

"Yes. That was the day they told me I was being removed from office."

"Oh . . ." she said. "But how could you stop yourself from telling me? Why didn't you say anything?"

"I didn't want to depress you before it was absolutely necessary. I was still hoping against hope, since I'd been told to stay in the capital while the denunciation was being examined. But that faint hope gradually faded away . . . Apparently the denunciation has been accepted."

"But why? Why?" she repeated, stifling a scream.

She looked at his grey-clouded eyes as if she could find in them the reason for the unfurling of the whole ghastly story.

"You're asking me why?" he said with a faint and bitter smile. "I don't consider myself to have eyes more clairvoyant than others, I can't see better or further into the future, and if I could I would be instantly suspect in the eyes of any tyrannical power . . ."

Good God! she thought. One evening her father had come out with the same thing, almost word for word.

"So, I don't count myself particularly clear-sighted. But there's a good reason for our sight to be extinguished. Every trace has to be destroyed."

"What? I don't understand."

"It's very simple. We were witnesses to many things that have to be wiped out."

"Who is we?"

"All of us who up to last night worked in the blinding commissions. Our eyes saw so many things they should not have . . . Do you understand?"

"Things you should not have seen," she repeated in a trailing voice. "Horrible things?"

"Of course. We were too close to the machinery, we were almost brushed by its cogs and belts."

"My poor darling." She sighed, and once again he felt her tears on his cheek, but the thought of the acid hurt him less acutely this time, as if his skin had already grown less sensitive to it.

"Sometimes lists were brought to us that had already been approved by higher authority," he said. "Investigations were only made retrospectively."

"What an abomination! In other words, all that gossip about the settling of scores wasn't that far off the mark?"

He nodded.

She snuggled up even closer to him. "What about the others?" she asked a moment later. "Is everyone who worked there going to meet the same fate?"

"Probably not. The first batch to be struck down are people who are suspected of being able to talk."

"Able to talk?" she repeated. "So what have eyes got to with that? The main requirement is the mouth . . ."

"The mouth's turn may come next," he cut in.

After a pause he added: "At any rate, if putting out eyes isn't sufficient to make a man see reason . . ."

"My God!" She sighed.

"In any case, even if none of us had been suspected, some would have been sacrificed automatically."

She stared at him with the awkward look of someone who has simply not understood what has been said.

"That's almost certainly one of the main reasons," he continued. "We're being sentenced so that a part of the horror of what happened gets attributed to us. Do you see what I mean? Everyone would like to put the blame for his own misfortune on us and our so-called mistakes . . ."

In the silence that followed each could hear the other breathing.

"As soon as they began to talk of the commission's mistakes," she said, "I felt my heart sinking, but then I tried to put the thought out of my head."

"Well, when those first rumours surfaced, my partner in the office said: 'It's our turn now'."

Silence ensued once more, and nothing could be heard except the rustling of their bodies as they tried to find another position in which to hold each other tight.

"Was it just a coincidence, or was that why you asked me the other day about the Köprülüs?"

"No, it wasn't coincidental at all. I could pretty much guess what you were going to say. I knew all too well that the Köprülüs have their own troubles to worry about. But a drowning man tries to pull himself out of the water by his own hair, if that's all there is to grab!"

"Now I understand why my mentioning making love in the dark made you go on and on, like a man in a fever, saying, 'In the middle of the night, in the dark . . .'"

"Yes. I'd already begun to feel I belonged to the world of the night."

She stroked him for a long while. "As long as I'm here you'll belong to this world, the world of light."

The grey shadow in his eyes was imbued with boundless suffering.

"Do you think there's no hope at all?" she inquired. "Isn't there any way to plead your case?"

He shook his head.

"Where do they do the investigations? Where are such decisions made? In your case, for example."

"Nowhere, in all likelihood. The decision may have been made on day one, as soon as the poison-pen letter about me came in . . ."

"Of course . . . All trace has to be erased . . ."

She thought better of asking any more pointless questions and went back to cuddling him. He barely responded to her comforting caresses. But his eyes remained alert, with a kind of morbid gleam. He gazed hungrily at her breasts, at the blue marks on her upper thigh, at her belly, then still lower, between her legs, which she spread open so he could more easily see her sex.

He's looking at me like that so he can memorise it completely, she thought.

"I shall live with your image engraved in my mind," he said, as if he had read her thoughts.

"I'll wait for you," she replied in a flattened voice. "Do you understand? I'll wait for you to come back from that place . . . I'll live only for you. If you don't keep me engraved in your memory as I am today, I think I'd die . . . I would fade away like a shadow . . . I would lose all life and shape . . . I remain the same as you remember me. Only if you consciously blot me out of your mind will I truly disappear, like a drawing rubbed out by an eraser . . ."

He didn't reply but only went on slowly stroking the part of her body he had been gazing at so insistently a few minutes before. She noticed that as he moved his hand over her he kept his eyes shut. He's imagining what it will be like to caress me when he's not able to see, she thought.

She was on the point of bursting into tears and screaming like a madwoman, not only at the thought of the misfortune about to descend upon her, but also, and above all, for a reason she couldn't even admit to herself but which surged up in confusion from the depths of her being: the fear of not being able to keep the promise she had just made Xheladin.

"What if I put out my eyes at the same time?" she asked suddenly, as if she'd been struck by a burst of fever. "On a bright morning, on the verandah, it couldn't be easier . . . That way we would both belong to the same side of the world . . . Then even if I wanted to I wouldn't be able to leave you . . ."

Her words were then smothered in tears, and he couldn't make out what she said at the end.

"Don't be so stupid!" he said kindly. "You said such sensible things a moment ago. What's made you talk so crazy now?"

They hugged again, and then he said: "We can be together as night and day. I will be your night, and you will be my day . . . All right?"

She sobbed so hard she couldn't answer. She tried to hold back her tears, but instead burst into heart-rending hiccups of the sort that go with weeping over an irreparable loss.

11

By all visible evidence, the campaign was winding down. Admittedly, town criers hadn't come back to the squares to proclaim a return to normal, but everyone was convinced the scourge had passed. Here and there, it could still strike someone down, like the last streak of lightning at the end of a storm, but its flashes were now enfeebled and far away.

The last days of autumn were slowly turning into ordinary days, the way they had been before the *qorr-firman*. One by one, the blinding offices had been closed, and to many people it seemed as if they had never existed. Cafés were full of customers once more, and their faces glowed with the joy of having escaped blind fate. Ghastly words like *misophthalmia*, *qorrof-fice*, *Tibetan*, which, when first heard long before seemed destined to mark out life's path to all eternity, were now dropped and forgotten.

The marks on Marie's white legs also gradually disappeared. She thought that was probably how her own image would fade in her fiancé's mind.

God knew what he was doing, with his hands and feet tied in some dark dungeon. They tied them up like that, so people said, as they did with men condemned to death, to stop them tearing off their blindfolds.

One of their acquaintances had spoken to them about what it was like to live in a dungeon. Prisoners spent daylight hours half-reclining, lying side by side in long rows. Some prayed nonstop, others wept, some silently, some sobbing out loud. Some talked to themselves for hours on end. Others revolted, yelled out like men possessed, swore at the accursed decree, and ended up calming down and asking for forgiveness, beseeching mercy, and begging Allah to grant long life to the emperor. And then there were those who went into a religious trance and looked forward to the day of their blinding so they would be freed, in their own words, from the sight of this sub-lunar world.

Some became delirious, and in a kind of ecstasy made speeches lasting hours on end. The world, they would say, looked more beautiful now that they could no longer see it, and far from suffering from the dark, they could feel their heads fill to the brim with light. They claimed they at last understood that eyes do not allow light to enter human minds, but on the contrary, like taps installed back-to-front, let inner light leak out and thus impoverished the mind.

That's what one kind of prisoner said, but most of them remained silent, as if they had been struck dumb. Now and then, they would wave their bound arms about incomprehensibly, as if they were clearing a cobweb away from in front of their blindfolded eyes.

God alone knew what Xheladin was doing! Had he kept her image intact in his memory? Or had that shape already begun to grow faint?

Marie instinctively put her hand to her cheek and her lips, as if the decomposition of her image could affect her physically. Then she stared at her body, where the blue marks had been, but had now almost vanished, and was overcome by gloomy thoughts on the ephemeral nature of all things.

She had told him she would wait, but she knew that was not entirely true. To be sure, she would wait for him in her thoughts, she would never forget him, but that was not the same thing at all. The first Sunday without him, when the family at table fell into a funereal silence, they all came to the conclusion that he was now in that place whence no man returns: she also convinced herself that it was all over between them.

The last and only piece of news they had about him was that his request to the authorities to be blinded in the European manner had been accepted.

"No point thinking about him again," her father said. "You're too young to spend the rest of your life with a blind man. In addition, you know full well that it's not a blindness inflicted by disease or an act of God, but by the will of the state . . ."

She did not answer but went up to her room to mourn her separation in silent sobs.

Deep inside her heart, she felt immense joy at having given herself to him entirely. She could not have done more.

Winter was coming on with its miserable and endless nights, and she felt that henceforth he would really be her night, her uneasy sleep, her eternal regret. Sometimes she imagined that a similar feeling of guilt hung in the air, borne by winter's first winds, and rattling in the windowpanes and the other sounds of ordinary life.

12

In early winter, the sightless suddenly began congregating on sidewalks and in cafés. Their fumbling steps caused passersby to stop and stare in disbelief. Although citizens had lived for months in fear of the *qorrfirman*, the sight of its results rooted them to the ground, petrified them.

For some time people had allowed themselves to think that the victims of that notorious order had been swallowed up in the dark night of oblivion, that the only people you would come across in the street or the square were the formerly blind, with their unchanging appearance, the peaceful tap-tap-tap of their sticks — the kind of blind people everyone's eyes and ears were long accustomed to. But now the first winter freeze had brought with it innumerable blind folk of a new and far more lugubrious kind.

There was something specific about them that

distinguished them from the traditionally unsighted. They had a disturbing swagger, and their sticks made a menacing knock-knock-knock on the cobblestones.

They've not yet grown used to their new condition, some argued. Blindness came to them at a stroke, not gradually, as is usually the case, so they haven't yet acquired the necessary reflexes . . . But those who heard such remarks shook their heads, clearly not convinced. Could that be the only reason?

What was most striking was their collective reappearance. It was probably not a coincidence, nor could it have been the result of secret collusion among them, contrary to the rumours that were being circulated by people who saw anti-state conspiracies in everything and anything. It came from the simple fact that the time needed for most of them to recover — either from the physical wounds caused by disoculation or from its attendant psychological trauma — had now elapsed.

Some among them, particularly those who had been blinded in the aristocratic manner, by exposure to the sun, bore a grave and dignified air as they went and sat down in cafés and tearooms. It was presumably easier for them to behave with hauteur, not just because of the cash bonus and the generous pension they had been granted but because their eyes had not been physically mutilated when they were blinded. On the other hand, most of the others had let themselves go. They were dressed in rags, and by way of footwear all they had were wooden clogs, which made the sound of their approach particularly distressing.

But those who had been unsighted by violent means were not the only ones to look wretched. Even some who had turned themselves in to the *qorroffices* and been received with all due honour were now shuffling around in tatters. Similarly, there were a number of well-dressed people — better dressed than they had been before — among those who had been disoculated violently. They stood defiantly in full sight of all, as if to challenge the world with their black and empty sockets.

At the sight of these gaping wounds, some people were so disturbed they themselves began to stumble, as if the ground had suddenly opened up beneath them.

Why do they have to show themselves like that? people wondered. Why aren't they forbidden access to main roads, to stop them curdling our blood with those ghastly holes in their heads?

The blind paid not the slightest heed to remarks of that kind. Not content to stay at tearoom and café tables for hours on end, they listened to the news read aloud from papers at nearby tables, and joined in the conversation. Fortunately, public affairs were taking a better turn nowadays, they would say, proving that their sacrifice had not been in vain. What a pity we can't see what's going on! some of them lamented over and over again. But that doesn't really matter in the end. Even if we can't see, we can imagine what it's like, and we're just as pleased about it as you are.

Some of them remained silent, black as crows, while others, taking up the tradition of the blind, got hold of a musical instrument and accompanied themselves as they sang epic rhymes or love songs of their own composition.

The tide of the blind continued to rise, at the same rate as hostile gossip about them. Rumour had it that a forthcoming decree would resettle most of them in some remote province of the country (the Empire wasn't short of impoverished regions of that kind!) so that foreigners, at least, would never set eyes upon them.

Far from giving any substance to such rumours, on the last Friday in December — on the very day when a special order was announced granting a full pardon to people blinded by violent means — the state held a Banquet of Forgiveness (a *sadaka*, as it was expressed in the language of the land) for the benefit of all the victims of the Blinding Order.

This "Reconciliation Banquet", as it was subsequently dubbed by malicious tongues, was held in the Imperial Manège, which was the only building large enough for the number of tables required for the many thousands of guests.

The blind flocked towards the manège from all quarters of the capital in an unending clatter of clogs and sticks, and in such confusion that the police were obliged to close the entire area to traffic for several hours.

Dozens of functionaries were there to welcome them and lead them to their places, but all the same, when the blind finally entered the Great Hall and especially when they tried to get to their designated tables, things degenerated into a veritable riot. They knocked over chairs, they did not know where to put the Balkan lyres and *lahutas* which they had brought with them, God knows why, most of them groped clumsily at their dinner plates and spilled food on themselves, or else tipped the plates right over.

Among this crowd of the blind, someone noticed

a clog-wearing, raggedy man elbowing his way towards a table, who was none other than the former grand vizier.

At a long table sat the high officials of the court, together with members of the government and of the entourage of Sheikh ul-Islam. Journalists and foreign diplomats had also been invited.

One of the officials tried to make a speech, but as most of the blind had begun to stuff themselves with food, most of his words were drowned by the scraping of cutlery and the clatter of crockery. Nonetheless, the essential sentences about the need for sacrifice in service of the common good, and especially the message from the sultan encouraging everyone to forget the past and remain loyal to the state, were relatively well understood.

With gravy dripping from their chins, and in high spirits induced by such good food — especially the nut halvah — many of the blind started strumming on their *lahutas*.

The officials, journalists and diplomats looked on in silence as the disorderly feast unfolded before their eyes.

"*Every cloud has a silver lining* . . . I think you

must have a similar saying in your language too," the Austrian consul eventually said to his colleague from France.

"Yes, of course," the Frenchman replied.

"In spite of its ghastly and untranslatable name, and even in spite of the notorious horror it has caused, the Blinding Order has contributed to a new flowering of oral poetry, which, as I myself noticed, has been in sharp decline in this country in recent years."

"Do you really think so?" the Frenchman replied, looking at his colleague in astonishment. Then he recalled that his colleague had once told him he was engaged in research on oral poetry, which made his remark seem less cynical than bizarre.

"Just look at this crowd, if you want to see the evidence," the Austrian added.

"I guess so," the French consul muttered, as he gazed into the Great Hall where the cacophony of the blind was rising to its peak.

Tirana, 1984

The Great Wall

Inspector Shung

Barbarians always go back over in the end. My deputy sighed as he spoke those words. I guess he was staring into the far distance, where their horses could just be seen.

For my part, I was reflecting on the fact that no-where in the vast expanse of China, not in its small towns, nor its large cities, nor in the capital — although people there do know more than provincials — nowhere can you find a single soul who fails to com-ment, when nomads go over the Wall (even nomads that go over as part of an official delegation), *Barbar-ians always go back over in the end*, while releasing a sigh of the sort usually given in response to events you imagine you'll eventually look back on with fond sadness.

It's been as quiet as the grave around here for decades. That does not stop our imperial subjects from imagining an unending brutal conflict, with the Wall on one side and the northern nomads on the other, both forever hurling spears and hot pitch at each other and tearing out eyes, masonry and hair.

But that no longer surprises me very much, when you think that people don't just bedeck the Wall with false laurels of valour, but envision all the rest of it — its structure, even its height — quite differently from the way it really is. They can't bring themselves to see that though there are places where the Wall is quite high — indeed, sometimes so high that if you look down from the top, as we could do right now from where we're standing, you become quite dizzy — along most of its length the Wall's dismal state of repair is a pity to behold. Because it has been so long abandoned, because its stones have been filched by local people, the Wall has shrunk: it barely tops a horse and rider now, and in one sector it's a wall only in name, just lumps of masonry scattered around like the remains of a project that got dropped for God knows what reason. It's in this kind of shape, like a snake you can hardly make out as it slithers through the mud, that the Wall reaches the edge of the Gobi Desert — which promptly swallows it up.

My deputy's eyes were blank, like the eyes of someone required to stare into the far distance.

"We're now awaiting an order," I said, before he

could ask me first what we ought to do next. It was obvious that the result of the negotiations with the official delegation of nomads would determine what that order would be — if any decision of the kind were ever made at all.

We waited for the order all summer long, then until the end of the summer-house season, when the emperor and his ministers were supposed to be back in the capital. The autumn winds came, then the snow-flecked drizzle of winter, but still no decision reached us.

As always happens in cases of this kind, the order, or rather its reverberation, arrived just when everybody had stopped thinking about it. I call it a reverberation because, long before the imperial mail reached us, we learned of the government's decision from the people living in the villages and camps strung out along the line of fortifications. They deserted their homes and resettled in the caves in the nearby hills, as they did every time news reached them, by means entirely mysterious, even before we were informed of impending repair work on the Great Wall.

It was probably a wise move on their part, since by making off to the hills, they would spare themselves the officials' whip, at the very least, not to mention many other punishments of every kind. I'd never understood why they constantly take masonry from the Wall to build their hovels and yards, knowing full well that they would have to bring it back to rebuild the Wall.

The process, they tell me, has been going on for hundreds of years. Like the skein of wool used to make a scarf — which is then unpicked to knit a sweater, which is then undone to knit another scarf, and so on — the Wall's great stones have made the return trip many times from peasant hovel to Wall and back again. In some places, you can still see streaks of soot, which predictably fire the fantasies of tourists and foreign plenipotentiaries, who can't imagine that the marks are not the trace of some heroic clash but only smoke stains from hearths where, for many a long year, some nameless yokel cooked his thin and tasteless gruel.

So when we heard this afternoon that the peasants had abandoned their dwellings, we guessed that the whole of China had already heard news of the call to rebuild the Wall.

Although it was a symptom of heightened tension, the repair work did not yet add up to war. Unlike armed conflict, rebuilding was such a frequent occurrence that the Great Wall's middle name could have easily been *Rebuilt*. Generally speaking, it was less a wall in any proper sense than an infinite succession of patches. People went so far as to pretend that it was in just such a manner the Wall had come into being in the first place — as a repair job on an older wall, which was itself the remaking of another, even older, wall, and so on. The suggestion was even made that at the very beginning the original wall stood at the centre of the state; but from one repair to another, it had gradually moved ever closer to the border, where, like a tree that's finally been replanted in the right soil, it grew to such a monstrous size it terrified the rest of the world. Even people who could not imagine the Wall without the nomads sometimes wondered whether it was their presence that had led to the building of the Wall, or whether it was the Wall rising up all along the border that had conjured up the nomads.

If we had not seen the coming of the Barbarian delegation with our own eyes, and then seen it going again, we might have been among the few who would have attributed this rise in tension (like most previous events of this kind) to the disagreements that frequently flare up inside the country, even at the very centre of the state. Smugly content to know a truth lost in an ocean of lies, we would have spent long evenings constructing all kinds of hypotheses about what would happen next and about the plots that could have been hatched in the palace, plots with such secret and intricate workings that even their instigators would have had a hard time explaining them, or emanating from jealousies so powerful that people said they could shatter ladies' mirrors at dusk, and so on and so forth.

But it had all happened under our noses: the nomads had come and gone beneath our very feet. We could still recall the polychrome borders of their tunics and the clip-clop of their horses' hooves — not forgetting the expression *"Barbarians always go back over in the end"* uttered by my deputy, along with his sighs and his blank stare.

In any other circumstance we could have felt, or at least feigned, a degree of doubt, but this time we realised there were no grounds for such an attitude. However tiresome winter evenings may be, we could find better ways of filling them than fabricating alternative reasons for the state's anxiety apart from the coming of the Barbarians.

*   *   *

A vague feeling of apprehension is coming down to us from the northlands. Right now the issue is not whether this state of heightened tension derives from the existence of a real external threat. From now on, and this is more than obvious, the only real question is whether there really will be war.

The first stonemasons have arrived, but most of them are still on the road. Some people claim forty thousand of them are on their way; others give an even higher figure. This is definitely going to be the most important restoration of the last few centuries.

The call of the wild goose awakes the immensity of the void. Yesterday, as I was looking out over the wastes to the north, this line from a poet whose name I forget came back to me. For some time now, fear of the void has been by far the greatest form of apprehension I feel. They say the nomads now have a single leader, a successor to Genghis Khan, and that amid the swirling confusion and dust that is the Barbarians' lot, he is trying to set up a state. For the time being we have no details about the leader except that he is lame. All that has reached us here, even before the man's name, is his limp.

These last few days, nomads have been emerging

from the mist like flocks of jackdaws and then vanishing again. It's clear that they're keeping an eye on the repair work. I am convinced that the Wall, without which we could not imagine how to survive, is for them an impossible concept, and that it must disturb them as deeply as the northern emptiness troubles us.

Nomad Kutluk

I've been told to gallop and gallop and never stop watching over it, but it's endless and always the same, stone on stone, stone under stone, stone to the left, stone to the right, all bound in mortar, however much I gallop, the stones never change, always the same, just like that damn snow that was always the same when we chased Toktamish across Siberia at the end of the Year of the Dog, when Timur, our *Khan kuturdilar*, told us: "Hold on in there, men, because it's only snow, it's only pretending to be cold like a conceited bitch, but just you wait, it'll turn soft and wet before long." But this army of stones is much more harmful, it won't flake or melt, and it's in my way, I don't understand why the Khan doesn't give us the order to attack that pile of rubble and take it down, the way we did at Chubukabad when we laid our hands on the Sultan Bayazed Yaldrem and the Khan sent us this *yarlik:* "Honour to you who have captured Thunder, no matter that you have not yet handcuffed the heavens entire, but that will come"; then, like at Akshehir during the Year of the Tiger when we buried our prisoners alive, all bent double as in their mothers' wombs, the *Khan kuturdilar* told us: "If they're innocent, as Qatshi the Magician believes, then Mother Earth, whose womb is more generous that that of a woman, will give them a second birth." Oh! those were the good times, but our Khan hasn't sent any more *yarliks* asking us to raze everything to the ground, and the chiefs, when they assemble to hold a palaver in the *kurultai*, claim that what people call towns are only coffins we must be careful never to enter, because once you're in you can never get out, that's what they say, but still the *yarlik* of destruction keeps on failing to come, all I get is that never-ending order over and over again just like the accursed stones: "Nomad, keep watch!"

Inspector Shung

Repair work is apparently proceeding along the entire northwestern stretch of the Wall. Every week parties of stonemasons arrive, gaily flaunting the many-coloured flags and banners from their province (the regions of the Empire compete with each other to send the largest work detail to the Wall), but nowhere can any troop movements be seen. Nomad lookouts flit across the horizon as before, but because the fog has thickened in the winter season, we often cannot make them out very clearly, neither the rider nor the horse, so that they look less like horsemen than mutilated body parts from who-knows-which battlefield whipped by wild gusts of wind into a flying swarm.

What is happening is like a puzzle. At first sight, you might think it a mere manoeuvre, each camp trying to show its strength by displaying contempt for the other. But if you consider matters with a clear mind, you can see they contain perfectly illogical elements. I do believe it is the first time there has ever been such a gap between the Wall and the capital. I had always imagined they were indissolubly connected, and that was not only when I was working in the capital, but even before then, when I was a mere minor official in the remotest valleys of Tibet. I always knew they had tugged on each other the way they say the moon does on the tide. What I learned when I came here was that while the Wall is able to move the capital — in other words, it can draw it towards itself or else push it farther away — the capital has no power to shift the Wall. At most, it can try to move away, like a fly trying to avoid the spider's web, or else come right up close so as to nestle in its bosom, like a person quaking with fear; but that's all it can do.

In my view, the Wall's forces of attraction and repulsion are what explain the movements of the capital of China over the last two centuries — its shift to the south of the country, when it went to Nanking, as far away from the Wall as possible, and then its return to the north, to the closest possible location, when it came back to Beijing, which for the third time assumed its role as China's capital city.

I have been racking my brains these last few days trying to find a more accurate explanation for what is going on at the moment. Sometimes I think the wobble, if I can use that word, results directly from the proximity of the capital. Orders can be countermanded more easily than if the capital were, say, four or five months away — when the second carriage bearing news of the cancellation of the order either fails to catch up with the first carriage or, because of excessive speed or its driver's anxiety, the carriage tips over, or else the first one crashes, or they both do, and so on.

Yesterday evening, as we were chatting away (it was one of those exquisitely relaxed conversations that often arise after time spent hidden from the view of others and thus seem all the more precious), my deputy declared that if not only the capital but China herself were to move, the Wall would not budge an inch. "And what's more," he added casually, "there is proof of what I say." Indeed, we could both easily recall that in the one thousand or so years that have elapsed since the Wall was built, China has more than once spilled out over its borders, leaving the Wall all alone and without meaning in the midst of the grey steppe, and it has shrunk back inside the same number of times.

I remembered an aunt who in childhood had had a bracelet put on her arm, a bangle. As she grew plumper, the bracelet, forgotten but left in place, became almost buried in her flesh. It seemed to me that something of the same kind had happened to China. The Wall had alternately squeezed her tight, and loosened its grip. For some years now, it had seemed about right for her size. As for the future, who could say? Each time I saw my aunt, I recalled the story of her bangle, which continued to obsess me. I really don't know why I could not stop thinking of what would have happened if the bangle had not been taken off in time, and, taking things to their limit, I could hear it jangling incessantly after her death, hanging all too loosely on the wrist of her skeleton . . . I lay my head in my hands, embarrassed at having imagined China herself decomposing with a trivial adornment around her wrist.

It was a starless night, but the moonlight gave off such a strong sense of indolence that you could believe that in the morning everyone would abandon all activity — that nomads, birds and even states would lie flat out, exhausted, as lifeless as corpses laid out beside each other, as we two then were.

We have at last learned the name of the nomad chief: he is called Timur i Leng, which means Timur the Lame. He is said to have waged a fearsome war against the Ottomans, and after having captured their king — called Thunder — had him paraded from one end of the vast steppes to the other.

Apparently, before long he'll be going after us next. Now it is all becoming clearer — the order for the rebuilding of the Wall, as well as the temporary calm which we all hastened to describe as a "puzzle", as we do for anything we can't understand in the workings of the state. While he was dealing with the Turks, the one-legged terror did not constitute a threat. But now . . .

A returning messenger who stopped here last night brought us disturbing news. In the western marches of our Empire, right opposite our Wall and barely a thousand feet from it, the Barbarians had built a kind of tower, made not from stone but from severed heads. The edifice as it was described to us was not tall — about as high as two men — and from a military point of view it was no threat at all to the Wall, but the terror those heads exude is more effective than a hundred fortresses. Despite the meetings with soldiers and stonemasons, where it was explained that the pile was, in comparison to our Wall, no more significant than a scarecrow (the crows that nonetheless swarmed around it had actually suggested the comparison), everyone, soldiers included, felt the wind of panic pass through them. "I've never had so many letters to take to the capital," the messenger declared as he patted his leather saddlebag. He said most of the epistles had been penned by officers' wives, writing to their aristocratic lady friends to report intolerable migraines and so forth, which was a way of asking them to please see if they could get their husbands transferred to another posting.

The messenger also said that the pestilential air that this pile of heads exhaled was so unbearable that for the first time in its existence the Wall had apparently contracted, and the messenger had prayed to God that the rebuilding work which had been launched at such an opportune moment should be completed as quickly as possible.

The messenger's tale left us all utterly depressed. Without admitting it to ourselves, we were aware that we would henceforth cast a quite different eye on the Wall's damaged parts, on its cracks and crumbly patches. Our minds obstinately kept turning towards the pile of severed heads. Once the messenger had left, my deputy pointed out that the wise old saying "Skull on stone breaks nothing but bone" — a phrase whose brushstrokes we mastered at primary school thanks to our teacher's liberal use of the rod — had become obsolete. The way things looked now, heads seemed more likely than anything else to be the weapon of choice against the Wall.

No troop movements on the border. A brutal earthquake has shaken everything except the Wall, which has long known how to cope with seismic disturbances. The silence that reigned after that last shock subsided seemed deeper than ever . . . I have the impression that the rebuilding work is being done none too carefully and just for show. The day before the quake, the building used as a watchtower, on our right, collapsed again, after having already been erected twice. It all leads me to think that treason has crept into the imperial palace. My deputy has a different view. He has long been convinced that people in the capital are so deeply immersed in pleasure and debauchery that few of them ever think of the existence of nomads and frontiers. Only yesterday he was telling me that he'd heard people say that a new kind of mirror has been invented — mirrors that more than double the size of a man's penis. Ladies take them into their bedchambers to arouse themselves before making love.

Our only comfort is that there doesn't seem to be the slightest movement on the other side of the Wall, except for a few scouts who flash past on horseback now and then, and sometimes we also see small groups of ragged Turkish soldiers. When, towards the end of summer, the Turks first appeared, our lookouts were terribly alarmed. Our first thought was that they might be attack units disguised as defeated Turks, but then we got reports from spies who had infiltrated them that they were in fact the remnants of the Ottoman army Timur had routed at Chubukabad. They've been wandering up and down the frontier for a long time now. Most of them are old men, and, when evening comes, their thoughts go back to those distant lands with fearsome names where they fought, and also presumably to their Sultan Bayazed, whose memory trails with them across the steppe like a dead flash of lightning.

More than once they asked for work on the Wall restoration project; after the repeated collapses of the right-hand tower, one was so persistent he actually got to see me personally and told me in bad Chinese that he'd once seen in a far distant land a bridge in one of whose pillars a man had been immured. He pointed to his eyes as he swore that he had really *seen* it, and even asked for a scrap of cardboard so he could draw the shape of the bridge for me. It was only a small bridge, he said, but to stop it from collapsing a sacrifice had to be made. How, then, could this huge Wall of China remain standing without an offering of the same kind?

He came back to see me a few days later and told the same story once more, but this time he made a detailed drawing of the bridge.

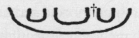

When I asked him why he'd pictured it upside down, he turned pale. "I don't know," he replied, "perhaps because that's the way it looks in the water . . . Anyway, the night before last, that's how I saw it in my dream. Upside down." After he left, we took some time to look at his bizarre sketch. He explained that the symbol † marked the place of the sacrifice. After I stared at it hard for a long while, I thought I could see the bridge beginning to quiver. Or was that because the Turk had told me that he remembered the bridge's reflection in the river better than the bridge itself? If I may say so, it was a way of seeing things from an aquatic point of view — a perspective, the Turk had explained, thought to diverge completely from a human point of view, for instance, or from a so-to-speak *terran* perspective. It was the waters that had demanded the sacrifice of immurement (at least, that's what the legend said) — that is to say, sentencing a man to death.

Late that night, slanting beams of moonlight falling on the masonry made human shapes appear here and there on the side of the Wall. "Accursed Turk!" I swore under my breath, believing it was he who had stirred up such morbid images in my mind. It then struck me that the upturned bridge was perhaps the very model of the way tidings good and bad move around our sub-lunar world. It was very likely that nations did indeed pass messages to each other in that way — signals announcing the coming of their official delegations, with their letters sealed with black wax, a few hundred or a few thousand years in advance.

Nomad Kutluk

The chiefs have gathered at the *kurultai*, and Khan Timur's *yarlik* has come: "Never venture over the other side," it says, "for that way lies your perdition." But the more I'm told not to, the more I want to step over and see the cities and the women who are doubled in burnished glass, wearing nothing but a gauze they call *mend-afsh* (silk), women with a pleasure-slit sweeter than honey, but this damned rock heap won't let me, it obstructs me, it oppresses me, and I would like to stab it with my dagger, though I know steel has no power over it, for it even withstood the earthquake only two days ago. When the shuddering earth and the masonry were wrestling with each other, I screamed aloud to the quake, "You're the only one that can bring it down!" But it made no difference, the Wall won out, it smothered the quake, and I wept as I watched the earthquake's last spasms, like a bull who's had its throat cut, until, alas, I saw it expire, and my God, did I feel sad, as sad as that other time in the plain of

Bek-Pek-Dala, when I said to the commander, Abaga, "I don't know why, but I feel like screaming," and he said, "This steppe is called Bek-Pek-Dala, the steppe of hunger, and if you don't feel your own hunger, you'll feel the hunger of others, so spur your steed on, my son." That's what they all tell me: spur your steed on, never let it stop, son of the steppe, but this lump of stone is stopping me, it's in my way, it's rubbing up against my horse, it's calling to its bones, and I myself feel drawn in to its funereal mortar, I don't know how, but it's made my face go ashen, it's making me melt and blanch, aaah . . .

Inspector Shung

The days drag along as wearily as if they had suddenly been broken by old age. We haven't yet managed to recuperate from the shock we had suffered at the end of this week.

Ever since his chariot halted at our tower and he said, "I am from Number 22 Department of Music," I have felt a foreboding of evil, or something very much like it. When I asked him what the role of his department was and whether he really meant to put on concerts or operatic pieces for the soldiers and workers on the Wall rebuilding project, he laughed out long and loud. "Our Department hasn't been involved in that sort of thing for ages!" What he then explained to us was so astounding that at one point my deputy interrupted him with a plaintive query: "Is all that really true, or is this a joke?"

We had of course heard that, over the years, some departments and sections of the celestial hierarchy, while retaining their traditional names, had seen their functions entirely transformed — but to learn that things had gone so far as to make supplying the emperor with sexual performance-enhancing drugs the main job of the navy's top brass, while the management of the fleet was now in the hands of the palace's head eunuch, well, nobody could easily have got their mind around that. But that's not the whole story, he said. "Do you know who's now in charge of the copper mines and the foundries? Or who's the brains behind foreign policy these days? Or the man in charge of public works?"

Our jaws dropped as, with smug satisfaction at his listeners' bewilderment, he answered his own questions, as if he were throwing old bones to hungry dogs. Lowering his voice, he confided that the institution now responsible for castrating eunuchs and for running the secret service was the National Library. Leaving us

no time at all to catch our breath, he went on to reveal that in recent times the clan of the eunuchs at
the imperial palace had seized an untold amount of
power. In his view they might soon be in complete
control of government, and then China might no
longer be called the Celestial Empire, or the Middle
Empire, but could easily come to be known as the Empire of Celestial Castration . . .

He guffawed for a while, then his face darkened.
"You may well laugh," he said, "but you don't realise
what horrors that would bring in its wake." Far from
smiling, let alone laughing, our expressions had turned
as black as pitch. Despite which, he went on prefacing
all his remarks with "You may well laugh, but . . ."
In his mind, we were laughing without grasping the
calamity that would come of it. Because we did not
know that emasculation multiplies a man's thirst for
power tenfold, and so on.

As the evening wore on, and as he drank ever
more copiously, especially towards the end, the pleasure of lording it over us and his pride in coming from
the capital pushed him to reveal ever more frightful
secrets. He probably said too much, but even so none
of his words was without weight, for you could sense
that they gave a faithful representation of reality.

When we broached the threat from the north, he snorted with laughter as thunderously as ever before. "War with the nomads? How can you be so naïve, my poor dear civil servants, as to believe in such nonsense? The Wall rebuilding project? It's got nothing to do with the prospect of battle! On the contrary, it's the first article of the secret pact with the Barbarians. Why are you looking at me with the glassy stare of a boiled cod? Yes, that's right, the repair work was one of the Barbarians' demands."

"Oh, no!" my deputy groaned, as he put his head between his hands.

Our visitor went on in a more measured manner. To be sure, China had raised the Wall to protect itself from the nomadic hordes, but so much time had passed since then that things had undergone a profound change.

"Yes," he said, "things have changed a lot. It's true China was afraid of the Barbarians for many a long year, and at some future time she may well have reason to fear them again. But there have also been periods when the Barbarians were afraid of China. We're in one such period right now. The Barbarians are afraid of China. And that's why they asked, quite firmly, for the Wall to be rebuilt."

"But that's crazy!" my deputy said. "To be afraid of a state and at the same time ask it to strengthen its defences makes no sense at all!"

"Heavens above!" our visitor exclaimed. "Why are you so impatient? Let me finish my explanation . . . You stare at me with your big eyes, you interrupt me like a flock of geese, all because you don't know what's at the bottom of it. The key to the puzzle is called: fear. Or to be more precise, it is the nature of that fear . . . Now, listen carefully, and get it into your heads: China's fear and the Barbarians' fear, though they are both called *fear* in Chinese, are not the same thing at all. China fears the destructive power of the Barbarians; the Barbarians fear the softening effects of China. Its palaces, its women, its silk. All of that in their eyes spells death, just as the lances and dust of the nomads spell the end for China. That's how this strange Wall, which rises up as an obstacle between them, has sometimes served the interests of one side, and sometimes the other. Right now it's the nomads' turn."

The thought of insulting him to his face or calling him an impostor, a clown and a bullshitter, left my mind for good. Like everything else he'd said so far, this had to be true. I had a vague memory of Genghis

Khan's conquest of China. He overthrew our emperors and put his own men in their place, then turned on those same men because they had apparently gone soft. Had Yan Jey, one of our ministers, not been convicted a few years back for having asserted, one evening after dinner, that the last four generations of the Ming dynasty, if not its entire ascendance as well, were basically Mongol?

So the repairs to the Wall had been requested by the Barbarians. Timur, with more foresight than his predecessors, had decided that invading China was not only pointless but impossible. What China loses by the sword it retakes by silk. So Timur had chosen to have the border closed, instead of attacking. This is what explains the calm that settled over both sides of the Wall as soon as the delegation came over. What the rest of us had ascribed so unthinkingly to an enigma, to frivolousness, even to a hallucination engendered by penis-enlarging mirrors, was actually the straightforward outcome of a bilateral accord.

That night a swarm of thoughts buzzed in my head. States are always either wiser or more foolish than we think they are. Snatches of conversation with officials who had been posted on the other side came back to me, but I now saw them in a different light.

The ghost of Genghis Khan has weakened, I used to hear from people who'd carried out espionage in the northlands. But we heard them without paying much attention, telling ourselves: These are just tales of the Barbarians. They've gone softer, then become hardened again, and taking that sort of thing seriously is like trying to interpret the shapes made by flights of storks in the sky. But that was not right at all. Something really was going on out there on the grey steppe, and the more I thought about it the more important it seemed. A great change was taking hold of the world. Nomadism was on its last legs, and Timur, the man whom the heavens had had the whimsy to make lame, was there to establish a new balance of power. He had brought a whole multitude of peoples to follow a single religion, Islam, and now he was trying to settle them in a territory that could be made into a state. The numerous incursions of these different nations, which had previously seemed incomprehensible, would now probably come to a halt on the surface of the earth, though it was not at all clear whether that was a good thing or bad, since you can never be sure whether a Barbarian contained is more dangerous than one let loose . . . I imagined Timur standing like a pikestaff at the very heart of Asia and all around him nomadic peoples barely responding to his exhortations to stop their wild forays . . .

From the high battlements, I could see a whole section of the Wall that the moonlight seemed to split open throughout its length. I tried to imagine Timur's reaction when he was first shown a sketch of it. Surely he must have thought: *I'll knock it down, raze it, plant grass over it so its line can never be recovered.* Then, pondering how to protect his monastically strict kingdom from the softening wind of permissiveness, he must have said to himself that Heaven itself could not have presented him with a gift more precious than that Wall . . .

Next day, before dawn, when our visitor mounted his chariot to be on his way, I was tempted to ask him just what the Number 22 Department of Music was, but for reasons I'm unsure of I felt embarrassed to do so. Not so much politeness, I think, as the fear of hearing some new abomination. "May you break your damn neck!" my deputy cursed as the four-in-hand clattered noisily away between two heaps of rubble. Feeling vanquished, we looked out over a landscape that, despite having sated our eyes for years on end, now looked quite different. We had cursed our guest by wishing his chariot would turn end over end, but in fact it was he who had already taken his revenge by turning our minds upside down.

So the Wall was not what we had thought it was. Apparently frozen in time and unmovable in place while all beneath it shifted with the wind — borders, times, alliances, even eternal China herself — the Wall was actually quite the opposite. It was the Wall that moved. More faithless than a woman, more changeable than the clouds in the sky, it stretched its stony body over thousands of leagues to hide that it was an empty shell, a wrap around an inner void.

Each day that passed was ever more wearisome, and we came to realise to what degree we had become part and parcel of the Wall. We cursed it as we felt, now that it had betrayed us, how much more suffering it was bringing us. Our visitor's prediction that the Wall would one day serve China again was a meagre consolation, as was the other view, namely that the Wall's inner changes were perhaps what constituted its real strength, for without them it would have been nothing more than a lifeless corpse.

When I looked at it in the early mornings, all covered with frost, I was overcome with gloomy thoughts. It would certainly survive us all. It would look just the same — grey and mysterious — even when all humanity had disappeared. It would rust on humanity's cadaver, like the bangle on my aunt who had been rotting six feet under for years.

The death of a nomad scout at the foot of the Wall woke us from our torpor. We had seen him now and again galloping ever closer to the Wall, as if he had been trying to stick to it, until he finally crashed straight into it like a sightless bird.

We did not wait for any instruction, but prepared ourselves to provide an account of the event to a commission of inquiry, from our own side or from the Barbarians'. As we examined the bloodstains streaked along the Wall over fifty feet and more (it seems that even after injuring himself the rider had spurred his horse faster and more furiously) my mind turned back to that far-off bridge that had been said to demand a sacrifice. Good Lord, I thought, can they have been in contact with each other so quickly?

I also mused about the distance that such a portent can cover, about the migration of forebodings and also, of course, about the mystery surrounding the image of the upside-down bridge. It was one among the hundreds of misleading images this world provides us with, which can only ever be seen in hindsight.

The Ghost of Nomad Kutluk

Now that I am on this side and no longer need a steed or any kind of bird to get around, since a breath of wind or even, on calm nights, a pale moonbeam will do the job for me — now that I am in the beyond I am no longer astounded by the thick-headedness of the people down below or by their infuriating narrow-mindedness.

That narrowness must surely lie at the root of their superficial judgment of all things, as is notably the case (to take only one instance of the stupid blunders I was unfortunate enough to encounter) of the Great Wall of China, to which people down on earth attribute huge importance, whereas it is in reality only a ridiculous fence, especially when you compare it to a real barrier like the true Wall, the Mother Wall, the one that makes all others pale into the insignificance of feeble copies, or, to call it, as many do, that bourne from where no traveller returns — the wall that comes between life and death.

So of course I no longer need a horse; similarly, foreign languages, learning, and all the other things understood to be part of civilisation are of no use to me now. Souls manage to communicate perfectly well without them.

That horrible fall into the abyss, which came just after I thrashed my feeble body like a rag on the kerb-stone of China, was enough to make me realise things it would have taken me thousands of years to under-stand down there. The knowledge taught by fear is in-comparably superior to the product of all civilisations and academies put together, and I think that is the main if not the sole reason why we are forbidden to re-turn, even for a day. It is probably thought that we would need barely a few weeks to become masters of the planet, and that would clearly not be to the taste of the gods.

Strange to say, although we spirits smile wryly as we talk of our mistakes, resentments, clashes and con-flicts of yore, most of us up here would still like to go back, even if for only a brief time. Some can't wait to denounce their murderers, others want to leak state secrets or to elucidate mysteries they took with them to the grave, but for most of us, it's plain nostalgia. Of course, our desire to see our nearest and dearest is also shot through with the wish to tell but the tiniest part of the wonders we have seen from this side.

Every ten or fifteen thousand years the rumour goes round that home visits are going to be allowed. The great mass of ghosts then starts to hurry towards the Wall. But then we see it looming before us, a great sinister mass in the darkness of the night. The lookouts are blind, so it is said. Crossings happen in one direction only, from there to here . . . never from here to there.

Buoyed by the whisper that one day there will be two-way travel through the Wall, we carry on hoping all the same. Some cannot hold back their tears. They claim they've been expected for all eternity by beings who are dear to them, or by temples where they would try to pour balm on wounded minds or even by whole nations that are dying to see them return. They say they have invitations, which they wave like banners from afar, certificates from people who say they're prepared to give them board and lodging and who will even stand surety for their safe return. They parade academic insignia topped by royal crowns, and other sacred stamps, occasionally of dubious origin. But the gates never open, not for anyone.

Spirits get angry, start to protest, and make a racket that can be heard at the top of the watchtowers.

They yell that it's the same old story as on earth, that nothing has changed, that it's just as strict, just as inhuman . . .

Since it is another case of crossing a boundary, we who have experience of walls and other kinds of barriers cherish the hope that we may be granted special favour. Sometimes we get together among ourselves: some show off the scars from the spears and bullets that went through them, others show the tears made in their skin by barbed wire, or the holes made in their chests by the tips of embassy railings. We imagine those wounds will suffice to soften the hearts of the guardians of the gate. But we soon realise those are just vain hopes and that no one will be granted a *laissez-passer*.

When the others see how we are being treated, they lose all hope. Small, defeated groups straggle away, reckoning that the laws will be relaxed one fine day, and they start to listen out once again for a new rumour to cheer them up.

Last time, in the waiting crowd, someone pointed out a fellow called Jesus Christ . . . They've been making every imaginable special case for him for all eternity, they even sing hymns in his honour. What's more, his emblem shining from the roofs of cathedrals shows that of us all over here, he is certainly the one most expected back on earth.

As a matter of fact, even he is not optimistic. He comes and goes at the base of the Wall, displaying from afar the marks of the nails with which they crucified him, but the guardians pretend not to see them. Unless, as we have long suspected, the guardians are truly eyeless.

Paris, Winter 1993

Ismail Kadare's Acceptance Speech for The Man Booker International Prize 2005

Mr Chairman, members of the panel, ladies and gentlemen:

Thank you, thank you with all my heart, for the great distinction you award me, and for the kind words that have been said.

There would be a grave risk of you thinking a writer who has travelled two thousand kilometres to be here a little simple-minded and banal if he were to begin his speech with a hymn declaring his faith in literature, and saying, more precisely, that literature is what made him a free man.

It's true that it is two thousand kilometres from Tirana, the capital of my country, to Edinburgh, the capital of Scotland. All the same, I shall not only make such a declaration of faith in literature, but however strange it may seem, I will also add that for me, at the very start, Scotland played a key role in understanding how freedom and literature relate to each other.

Allow me to summarize what I wrote forty years ago in one of my first books, *Chronicle in Stone*.

I was born and grew up in a small, medieval Albanian city overshadowed by a great castle, as daunting as it was impressive. All regimes had used the castle as a prison, and the Communist regime was no exception. As it could be seen from all parts of the city, the castle and its prison-tower radiated power and menace in every direction.

As a child I grew up in the shadow of that castle. When I was eleven or twelve, however, in the season of our first serious encounters with reading, another castle took over my mind and my imagination. It was a Scottish castle, located not so far from here: the castle of Macbeth.

My fascination with that distant northern castle was enough to make my local fortress fade into insignificance. Its prison and its prison guards and its menace all grew somehow blurrier. A very strange thing had come to pass. A teenager from the back end of a tiny country crushed under the heel of Communism – Albania – had been propelled, by force of Shakespeare, so to speak, towards the inaccessible shores of misty Scotland.

That teenager was already a citizen of another realm, the realm of literature. He had entrusted to it his imagination and also his moral conscience. Its laws came to override all other law. Its leaders – Homer, Shakespeare, Dante, Kafka – became his true masters.

I gave myself up to that fascination as to a religion.

The same question has been put countless times to people who, like me, are writers from the former Communist empire: "How do you account for the fact that, in those times, and in that place, where and when it seemed quite impossible to do so, you were nonetheless able to write real literature?" My own answer to that question usually goes like this: "We believed in literature. In return for our belief and our fidelity, literature granted us her blessing and protection."

Believing in literature means believing in a reality above that which is. Believing in literature means saying that the ghastly regime holding sway over your country is altogether insipid, compared to literature in all its funereal majesty.

Believing in that art means being convinced that the regime to which you are subjected, with its policemen who spy on you, its top leaders and its functionaries – in sum, that the entire edifice of tyranny is but a passing nightmare, something dead in comparison to the Supreme order whose disciple you now are.

To explain myself briefly, I'd like to refer you to an episode in the *Divine Comedy*. Dante Alighieri, as he travels through Hell, is frightened of a huge, oncoming storm. Dante's master, Virgil, tells him: "Be not afraid, for it is a dead storm!"

That phrase helps to clarify what I was just saying. If you can manage to make yourself see the rough weather of dictatorship as a "dead storm", you'll have the key to the enigma. But a writer can only get that key from literature.

When you are a writer, it is not easy to be aware of living in a regime of death. In the totalitarian system, literature and the other arts suffered an ordeal of unprecedented cruelty. Of course, writers have been punished in all eras, and censorship, prisons, deportation and exile have always existed. But the regime I am referring to was not content merely to ban the most famous works in the canon – the "cathedrals" of artistic creation. No, the regime tried to annihilate the very possibility of such monuments ever being built again. In other words, it tried to destroy the raw material from which such cathedrals are hewn. It did its best to create a new race of writers who then proceeded with enthusiasm to destroy literature by their own hand.

In a sense, Stalinism was a great success. The line of writers abandoning the Temple grew ever longer, whilst those who kept the faith and stayed put saw their number dwindle by the day. We were only a tiny minority in that boundless, hopeless desert called Socialist Realism.

We propped each other up as we tried to write literature as if that regime did not exist. Now and again, we pulled it off. At other times we didn't. The idea that we could create a few mouthfuls of spiritual nourishment for our imprisoned nation filled us with joy.

Let me stress this point: that modest spiritual nourishment was a kind of survival ration for our people in their prison-land.

And then, suddenly, one day, passing through the night of dictatorship, our prison bread ended up by accident on your table. In your free cities – Paris, London, New York, Madrid, Vienna, Rome? – you picked up the prison loaf and inspected it with curiosity. You took a bite and found it good, and reckoned it was just as edible by you who live in the free world.

An Albanian writer could not have imagined any higher kind of praise ever being given. For him it was a miracle of Biblical proportions. Tiny, forgotten, isolated Albania, a land that had almost been buried alive, had apparently shown a sign of continuing life. Albania had signalled that though bound hand and foot by dictatorship, it hadn't yet enslaved its soul.

That signal, broadcast by means of literature and so nobly picked up by you, my dear friends, is what has made the unthinkable possible. It's that signal which made today's prize possible. It's what enabled me to travel here, to far distant Scotland, and it's that little sign which will enable me to undertake a visit tomorrow to where my imagination first dwelt, to a house which, more than any other edifice, fired my passion for literature: the castle of Macbeth, Thane of Glamis and Cawdor.

We propped each other up as we tried to write literature as if that regime did not exist. Now and again, we pulled it off. At other times we didn't. The idea that we could create a few mouthfuls of spiritual nourishment for our imprisoned nation filled us with joy.

Let me stress this point: that modest spiritual nourishment was a kind of survival ration for our people in their prison-land.

And then, suddenly, one day, passing through the night of dictatorship, our prison bread ended up by accident on your table. In your free cities – Paris, London, New York, Madrid, Vienna, Rome? – you picked up the prison loaf and inspected it with curiosity. You took a bite and found it good, and reckoned it was just as edible by you who live in the free world.

An Albanian writer could not have imagined any higher kind of praise ever being given. For him it was a miracle of Biblical proportions. Tiny, forgotten, isolated Albania, a land that had almost been buried alive, had apparently shown a sign of continuing life. Albania had signalled that though bound hand and foot by dictatorship, it hadn't yet enslaved its soul.

That signal, broadcast by means of literature and so nobly picked up by you, my dear friends, is what has made the unthinkable possible. It's that signal which made today's prize possible. It's what enabled me to travel here, to far distant Scotland, and it's that little sign which will enable me to undertake a visit tomorrow to where my imagination first dwelt, to a house which, more than any other edifice, fired my passion for literature: the castle of Macbeth, Thane of Glamis and Cawdor.

Believing in that art means being convinced that the regime to which you are subjected, with its policemen who spy on you, its top leaders and its functionaries – in sum, that the entire edifice of tyranny is but a passing nightmare, something dead in comparison to the Supreme order whose disciple you now are.

To explain myself briefly, I'd like to refer you to an episode in the *Divine Comedy*. Dante Alighieri, as he travels through Hell, is frightened of a huge, oncoming storm. Dante's master, Virgil, tells him: "Be not afraid, for it is a dead storm!"

That phrase helps to clarify what I was just saying. If you can manage to make yourself see the rough weather of dictatorship as a "dead storm", you'll have the key to the enigma. But a writer can only get that key from literature.

When you are a writer, it is not easy to be aware of living in a regime of death. In the totalitarian system, literature and the other arts suffered an ordeal of unprecedented cruelty. Of course, writers have been punished in all eras, and censorship, prisons, deportation and exile have always existed. But the regime I am referring to was not content merely to ban the most famous works in the canon – the "cathedrals" of artistic creation. No, the regime tried to annihilate the very possibility of such monuments ever being built again. In other words, it tried to destroy the raw material from which such cathedrals are hewn. It did its best to create a new race of writers who then proceeded with enthusiasm to destroy literature by their own hand.

In a sense, Stalinism was a great success. The line of writers abandoning the Temple grew ever longer, whilst those who kept the faith and stayed put saw their number dwindle by the day. We were only a tiny minority in that boundless, hopeless desert called Socialist Realism.